ADDRESS: The Puppet Master's Caravan

AGE: ~~6, 20, 83, 140, 237,~~ About 400
(I know I am!)

MOBILE: 07713 122?
(Sneaked back off the pirates)

SCHOOL: St Beckham's
I'm too old for school!

THINGS I LIKE: Copter Fish broth;
Gorillas; swinging through trees;
my hammock aboard the 'Betty Mae';
practising cutlass fighting

THINGS I HATE: Joseph Craik (a bully);
Captain Cut-throat (a bully):
gizzards;

D1096670

Fantastic food for
explorers!

← Icicle.

Brrr! It's cold!

The AMAZING AdvenTurEs of <u>me</u> CHARLIE SMALL
(400 year-old boy adventurer!)

Notebook No. 3

THE PUPPET MASTER'S PRISON

RED FOX

CHARLIE SMALL JOURNAL 3: THE PUPPET MASTER'S PRISON
A RED FOX BOOK 978 1 782 95324 1

First published in Great Britain by David Fickling Books,
(when an imprint of Random House Children's Publishers UK
A Random House Group Company)

First published as *The Puppet Master* 2007

This Red Fox edition published 2014

3 5 7 9 10 8 6 4

**Penguin Random House is committed to a sustainable future for
our business, our readers and our planet. This book is made from
Forest Stewardship Council® certified paper.**

MIX
Paper from
responsible sources
FSC® C018179

Printed and bound in Great Britain by Clays Ltd, St Ives plc

Set in 15/17pt Garamond MT

Red Fox Books are published by Random House Children's Publishers UK,
61–63 Uxbridge Road, London W5 5SA

www.**randomhousechildrens**.co.uk
www.**totallyrandombooks**.co.uk
www.**randomhouse**.co.uk

Addresses for companies within The Random House Group Limited can be found at: www.
randomhouse.co.uk/offices.htm

THE RANDOM HOUSE GROUP Limited Reg. No. 954009

A CIP catalogue record for this book is available from the British Library.

If you find this book, PLEASE look after it. This is the only true account of my remarkable adventures.

My name is Charlie Small and I am four hundred years old, maybe even more. But in all those long years, I have never grown up. Something happened when I was eight years old, something I can't begin to understand. I went on a journey... and I'm still trying to find my way home. Now, although I have buried a deep-frozen corpse, burgled a house full of robbers and fought with a man three metres tall, I still look like any eight-year-old boy you might pass in the street.

I've travelled to the ends of the earth. I've fought terrifying battles and been attacked by blood-sucking bats! You may think this sounds fantastic, you could think it's a lie. But you would be wrong, because EVERYTHING IN THIS BOOK IS TRUE. Believe this single fact and you can share the most incredible journey ever experienced!

Charlie Small.

Invisible Enemies

A huge roar, like the howl of some gigantic beast, woke me with a start and made my heart hammer against my ribcage. I tried to open my eyes, but they were glued shut and I couldn't see a thing.

'Help!' I cried. 'What's going on?' The monster roared again, sounding very close and very angry, and I started to panic. I rubbed my eyes and felt something cold and gritty. What was it? I know . . . ice! My eyelashes had been fused together with ice.

I rubbed harder until, painfully, the ice started to pull away, taking most of my eyelashes with it. At last I could open my eyes. I expected a huge grizzly bear or a slavering giant lizard to be bearing down on me with wide, open jaws; but when I looked round all I could see was white. Everywhere and everything was completely white! The world was as blank as an empty piece of paper.

An empty
piece of paper!
↓

What was going on? Where was I? I could still hear the roars of an invisible animal all around me. My heart beat fast as I tried to work out what to do.

Then I noticed what looked like a pale sun above me. It was glimmering weakly, as if from a trillion miles away. Instinctively I reached out towards it, and was amazed to find that I could touch it! I giggled nervously. I could touch the sun; surely that wasn't right? What's more, it was freezing cold and . . . then I realized where I was. I was in a cocoon of snow and ice that had formed around me while I had been sleeping. What I thought was the sun was really just the daylight shining through the thinnest part of the roof of my ice shell!

I punched upwards through the false sun and stuck my head out of the hole. The roar of the

Looking out from my ice cocoon.

mystery animal was the roar of the wind; a violent wind, full of tiny shards of ice that stabbed my cheeks like needles. I ducked back down into my shelter. I wouldn't be able to go anywhere until the storm had died down so I decided to spend the time checking myself for any injuries I might have picked up during my escape from the pernicious Perfumed Pirates of Perfidy.

You can read about that in my second Journal – Pirate Galleon

Taking Stock

I still can't quite believe that I finally managed to escape my life aboard the pirates' ship, the *Betty Mae*, and leave behind my double-crossing, deadly shipmates! I'd tried and tried again to get away, but had always been thwarted at the last minute. I was forced to go on pirate raids, helping them steal bucketloads of treasure, and in the process I made a deadly enemy of the chief thief-taker, Joseph Craik.

I did learn some useful skills though. I am now a dab hand with a cutlass, I can tie a hundred different knots and have become such a good cook that if I could only find my way back home, I would surely be offered my own TV series; there can't be many chefs who know how to cook Seagull Beak Broth!

I then escaped with the help of a pompous, puffed-up puffer fish. The ridiculous fish had inflated itself into a hot air balloon, and we drifted across the wide Pangaean Ocean for a whole year. When we finally reached land, the puffer fish ran out of breath; we shot crazily over a mountain range and I landed, somehow fast asleep, in a drift of snow. I have no idea where the puffer fish is now, and can only hope that he is somewhere safe.

I've just opened my rucksack and emptied out its contents. I need to check my explorer's kit to make sure I haven't dropped anything on my long and precarious flight from the pirates. Luckily, it all seems to be there. My rucksack contains:

1) My multi-tooled penknife
2) A ball of string
3) A water bottle
4) A telescope
5) A scarf
6) An old railway ticket
7) This journal
8) My pyjamas (now rather tatty)
9) A pack of wild animal collector's cards
10) A glue pen (to stick any interesting finds in my book)
11) A big bag of Paterchak's mint humbugs (three quarters empty)
12) A slab of Kendal mint cake
13) A glass eye from the steam-powered rhinoceros

Humbugs (very strong!)

14) The remains of a huge slab of smoked whale meat that I took to eat on my journey
15) The hunting knife, the compass, the jungle map and the torch I found on the sun-bleached skeleton of a lost explorer
16) The tooth of a monstrous river crocodile
17) My mobile phone and wind-up charger which I managed to sneak back off Captain Cut-throat
18) A map of the Pangaean Ocean, useless to me now, but unquestionable proof of my fantastic journey!

So now I've finished checking my supplies, brought my journal up to date and repacked my trusty rucksack. Sticking my head out of the shelter again, the raw wind hit me like a slap in the face; but it has died down a little, and I really think it's about time I got moving.

Well, here goes; the sooner I start, the sooner I'll get home! I'll write more just as soon as I can.

Into White

It's been a long, wearying day, a day of complete terror and terrible confusion. But at least I can warm my frozen fingers and feet in front of an old wood-burning stove that I've found in a deserted hunter's lodge.

I had kicked away the ice shell that had formed around me and stood up . . . *Ooof!*

The cold wind hit me like a fist, knocking me straight back down again, but I struggled to my feet and then looked around. Oh no! It was no different from being inside my ice shelter!

Everything was covered in a thick layer of snow, with no tree or rock in the landscape to give me any idea of distance or scale. I pulled my coat tight around me and, glancing at the compass in my hand, set out in a westerly direction.

Perhaps my home was just a few miles away in the other direction, I don't know, but I had to go somewhere and west seemed as good a bet as any. At least I knew that by following my compass I wouldn't be trudging round and

round in circles, trapped on a featureless
expanse of ice forever!

I trudged through knee-high snow and
across huge frozen wastelands, watching my
compass needle all the while. The air was filled
with a billowing dust of snow and ice that
battered me constantly as I leaned into the
ferocious wind. My ears froze and my fingers
throbbed painfully with the cold. I was really
hungry after my year-long journey by
puffer-fish balloon, but I knew that if
I stopped to open my meagre rations,
I might well freeze to the spot. If I
was ever discovered, I would look like
a perfect ice-statue of a small eight-
year-old boy!

My ears froze!

I kept moving for hour after hour
and mile after mile until my brain was too cold
to make any sort of decision. I didn't have the
sense to stop and dig myself another shelter,
and I do believe that my journey would have
ended there and then in that ice-bound
landscape if, all of a sudden, the wind hadn't
dropped and the air cleared to reveal a weak
and watery sun. I would have cheered if my jaw
hadn't been frozen stiff, but I raised my

snow-encrusted arms in the air and shook them in triumph. Safe at last!

It was then that I heard a low and threatening growl coming from behind me. And this time it wasn't the wind!

The Chase

I turned round slowly. I was afraid that any sudden movement might startle whatever was behind me into making an attack.

The White Wolf

Inch by inch I shuffled around on the spot, until I found myself staring into the eyes of a huge, hunch-backed, pure white arctic wolf! It paced the ground restlessly, back and forth, about ten yards away. A low, constant growl rumbled in its throat as if it were powered by a diesel engine.

I took a tentative step forward, hoping to approach quietly and gain the wolf's trust by stroking its mighty white mane; but as soon as I moved, the wary creature slunk back and its growl erupted into a terrifying, deep-throated barking. The wolf pulled back its lips, exposing a mouthful of impressive teeth, the sort designed for ripping

flesh — it was, without any doubt, a wild and dangerous predator. How was I going to get out of this?

'Good dog, nice wolf,' I stuttered, backing slowly away. With every pace I retreated, the wolf took a pace forward, eyeing me warily. Great drools of saliva dripped from its jaws. It looked awfully mean and awfully hungry. I shuffled back and the wolf shuffled forward. This was hopeless; it was getting me nowhere. So I tried a different approach.

'SIT!' I yelled, and to my utter amazement the huge wolf parked its rear end in the snow and sat there. Fantastic! 'NOW STAY!' I ordered and took another pace backwards. The wolf stayed where it was! I took another step and another and still the wolf stayed put. When there was a good hundred yards between us, my nerve finally failed and I did what I had wanted to do from the very start. I turned and ran! I ran as fast as I could through the knee-deep snow. And the minute I started to run, the wolf was up off its haunches and streaking through the snow after me, howling like a banshee!

Dinner!

I knew that I'd had it as soon as the great white
wolf ran after me. He was bigger, meaner and
faster and as I clumsily stumbled through the
ever-deepening snow, the wolf streaked
through the drift as if he didn't exist.

'Help!' I cried as the wolf pounced, his front
paws hitting me in the back, knocking me face
down in the snow and pinning me to the
ground. '*Ooof!*'

The wolf snarled and growled, ripping at the
rucksack on my back in a mad frenzy. I closed
my eyes, dreading the snap of bone as he bit
into the back of my neck. Then the wolf's
snarls subsided into a happy whimpering as he
climbed off my back and dragged something a
little distance away. Nervously I raised my face
from the snow and turned to look.

Oh my goodness! The wolf was hunched
over a large slab of pink meat, tearing at it
greedily and keeping a suspicious eye on me at
the same time. Oh, help! I thought. The wolf
had sliced me open and removed a huge chunk
of my insides and was gobbling away as I

watched! But then why didn't I hurt anywhere?

Cautiously I felt my back and my neck. There were no obvious wounds, so what on earth was the wolf eating? I turned over and saw that my rucksack had been opened and its contents scattered across the snow. I gave a huge sigh of  relief when I realized that the wolf wasn't eating my liver; he was eating the slab of smoked whale meat that I had pinched from the *Betty Mae*.

Although that had been over a year ago, there was still quite a lot of the meat left, for the simple fact that it tasted disgusting; it was like a fish-flavoured, chewy jelly, and I had preferred to eat seaweed and cormorant's eggs on the long journey. The wolf seemed to be enjoying it though and had obviously been starving, because he was swallowing large chunks without even bothering to chew.

The wolf was gobbling away on a chunk of my insides!

I cautiously reached forward to where my animal collector's cards had been scattered across the snow. Maybe they would have something to say about the arctic wolf. Sure enough, I soon found the relevant card. This is what it said:

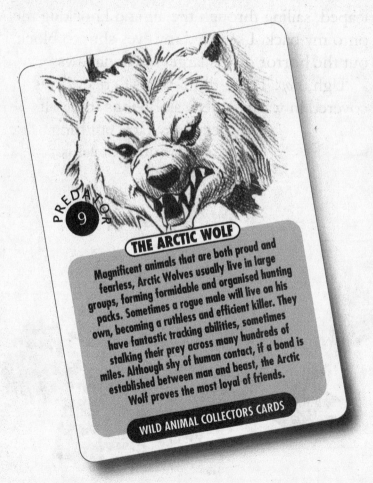

PREDATOR

9

THE ARCTIC WOLF

Magnificent animals that are both proud and fearless, Arctic Wolves usually live in large groups, forming formidable and organised hunting packs. Sometimes a rogue male will live on his own, becoming a ruthless and efficient killer. They have fantastic tracking abilities, sometimes stalking their prey across many hundreds of miles. Although shy of human contact, if a bond is established between man and beast, the Arctic Wolf proves the most loyal of friends.

WILD ANIMAL COLLECTORS CARDS

I finished reading just as the wolf swallowed the last chunk of whale meat, and as he looked across at me with his fierce, yellow eyes I couldn't see any sign of a bond between us. The wolf gave one gruff bark and raced towards where I sat in the snow. Once more he leaped, sailing through the air and knocking me onto my back. I screwed my eyes shut to block out the horror of his large, slavering jaws.

'Ugh, *stop*! That's disgusting!' I cried. I was covered in warm, smelly slobber as the wolf licked my face, emitting small quizzical yelps.

I opened my eyes and the wolf sat back and looked at me expectantly. What was going on? Why was I still sitting in the snow and not filling the belly of this wild and wicked wolf? It was then I noticed something around his neck – a collar!

I stretched out my hand and the wolf got up and walked cautiously towards me, until I could run my hand through his thick, white mane.

'Hello, boy,' I said, patting him on the flank. 'What's your name?' I felt for his collar through the thick mane of hair and discovered a small metal disc; scratched onto it was the word *Braemar*. 'Hello, Braemar, good lad,' I said ruffling his coat, and the wolf sidled up to me and laid his large head on my lap. 'You were just hungry, weren't you, boy?' I said. 'You weren't going to harm me. Now, if you have a collar, you must have an owner. Where's your owner, Braemar? Take me to your owner.'

The wolf got to his feet, barked at me and walked a few paces away. I quickly gathered my things from the floor, stuffed them back into my tatty rucksack and followed the wolf as he led me through the deep snow towards the featureless horizon.

Safe And Warm

We travelled for many hours, and as we walked, the snow started to fall again in large soft flakes, filling the air so completely that it was difficult to see Braemar as he trudged along ahead of me. Scared that I might lose him, I grabbed hold of his collar and let him lead me through the deep drifts.

The snow had blanked out the surrounding landscape so completely that I didn't notice the wooden shack until I tripped over its doorstep. Braemar had stopped and was looking from me to the hut, barking and whining. I scrambled to my feet as the wolf started pawing at the door. I was so cold that I didn't even bother to knock but ran into the hut as if I was bursting through my own back door at home.

'Hello,' I called, but there was no one home. A wood-burning stove stood against one wall of the hut and I rushed over and opened the metal door. The fire was out, but there was plenty of kindling wood stacked nearby, and a large box of matches sat on a shelf that was neatly stacked with tins of food.

I quickly laid a fire, hugging myself for warmth, and then touched a match to the kindling. It was very dry and the flames took hold immediately, crackling and spitting as I carefully piled on more wood. Soon I could feel the air start to warm and my frozen fingers and toes throbbed with pain as they began to

The Wooden shack.

thaw and the blood pumped through them once more.

'Thank you, Braemar,' I said, stamping my feet and rubbing my hands to ease the pins and needles. 'Thank you so much.' But Braemar was no longer at my side; he lay by some bunk beds at the far end of the hut. 'Come and get warm, boy,' I called, but the wolf didn't even look up. 'What's the matter?' I asked, reluctantly leaving the warmth of the stove for the gloom at the back of the room.

The wolf looked up at me with doleful eyes and then at the piles of blankets on the bottom bunk.

'What is it, boy?' I said as I lifted the corner of one of the covers. Oh my goodness! A human arm, stiff and sinewy, dropped down, slapping me across the knees.

'Yikes!' I cried, leaping back in shock. 'It's a body!' and I ran for the door.

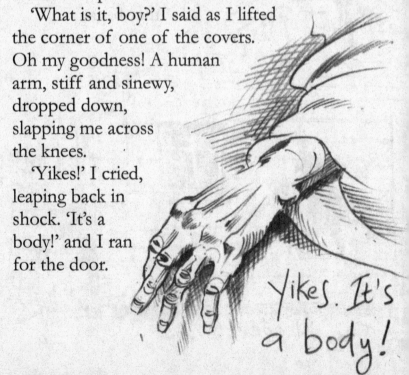

Yikes. It's a body!

The Trapper

Pull yourself together, I said to myself, once I had calmed down a bit. It can't hurt you . . . can it? I crept slowly back to the bunk beds, calling out 'Hello!' and 'Don't worry, I'm a friend,' but there was no reply from the heap of bedclothes.

I pulled the covers back in horror and, oh boy, I was right. There lay the body of Braemar's late master. It was impossible to say how long he had been there, for the cold had preserved his body. He was as deep frozen as a block of ice. The skin stretched over his face was thin and papery, a bit like the mummies I had seen on one of our museum trips at St Beckham's.

He was dressed in hunting clothes, his head topped with a large fur hat. A belt, which lay across his chest, was stuffed with knives of all shapes and sizes. He must have been a trapper, I thought, and these were the tools of his trade. Next to one of his hands was a piece of paper, and cautiously, not daring to breathe in case he moved again, I reached over and took it. It was a letter, the last wishes of a dying man. Still in shock, I read it with shaking hands. This is what it said:

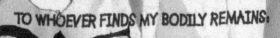

TO WHOEVER FINDS MY BODILY REMAINS:

The Old Hunting Lodge
Wind Blasted Ridge
Frozen Wastelands

Howdy Partner,

First I would like to apologise for giving you what must have been a terrible shock! I know I haven't got long for this world; I've been bedridden for a while now, suffering from the dreaded freeze that I picked up after falling through the ice into the frozen waters below. I managed to clamber out and normally I would have shrugged this chill off, but a combination of extreme old age and a very bad winter has meant that the infection has taken hold and I just can't shake it.

Never mind, partner; it's been a long and good life and I'm quite comfortable in my little hut. Soon I will be in those great trapping grounds in the sky, where, I believe, the beavers and the hairy squink shed their skins and leave them a-dangling on the branches of trees, and the rivers flow with pure whisky!

Please, help yourself to anything you may need, food or fuel, tools or arctic clothing. There are just three things I would ask you to do for me.

1) Please, bury me deep in a snowdrift close to my hut with my trusty hunting knives.

2) Send my faithful hunting companion, Braemar, back to the wild. Open the door and shoo him off. He will soon find a wolf pack to join up with, and it is by far the best thing for him.

3) When you leave, burn the hut down to stop Braemar returning and looking for me.

Good luck on your travels, whoever you are. You must be a long way from home to wind up in this frozen wasteland.

Bon voyage,

Archie Blane

Trapper Archie Blane

Well, I did what Trapper Blane asked. I dug a deep hole in the snow and gently laid the old man to rest, wrapped in his blankets. I found a piece of wood, wrote his name on  it and stuck it in the ground for a headstone.

It was a sad and unpleasant job, but shooing away Braemar was nearly more than I could manage. I gave him a good meal from the tins on Trapper Blane's shelf, then opened the door and chased him off, banging the empty tins together. The wolf looked at me, trying to understand why I was sending him away. Whether he understood or not I don't know, but all of a sudden he threw back his head and howled into the white sky. His cry echoed across the snow dunes and then faded. Then, in the distance another howl rose in the sky. Braemar looked at me once, barked, then shot off through the snow in the direction of the answering call.

'Goodbye, Braemar,' I shouted. 'And good luck!' The wolf did not turn round again, but carried on running until I could no longer distinguish his white fur from the snow-covered ground.

The Map

That evening I threw every available log into the stove, and soon the hut was warm and snug. I laid out my sodden clothes to dry in front of the fire, choosing some of Trapper Blane's cold-weather clothing to put on instead.

There was a cupboard full of trousers and jackets fashioned from fur and hides. I knew that animal trapping was not a nice thing, but as soon as I had pulled on the animal furs I realized how much more effective they were than my tattered jeans and trainers.

My fur clothes!

The trousers were a bit long but I could roll them up, and I stuffed some old paper into the boots that were a size too big and my toes were soon as warm as toast.

Now I have eaten my fill from the tins – Spam and baked beans, yum, the best meal I've had since leaving the *Betty Mae*! I've had a proper look around, and my heart leaped when I found a map among a lot of other notes and papers pinned to the wall of the hut; a map that shows a village maybe only a day's walk away. A village with proper houses and shops and people . . . And who knows, maybe there'll be a railway station with a train that could take me home! This is the very map that I have found.

Surely nothing can stop me now!

I was so pleased earlier, that I took my mobile from my pocket and phoned home. The line was full of static when Mum finally answered. For her it always seems to be the day that I left to go exploring, and she's still expecting me home for tea!

'Mum!' I cried when she answered the phone.

'Oh, hello, darling, is everything all right?'

'Well, things have been better, Mum! I'm in a

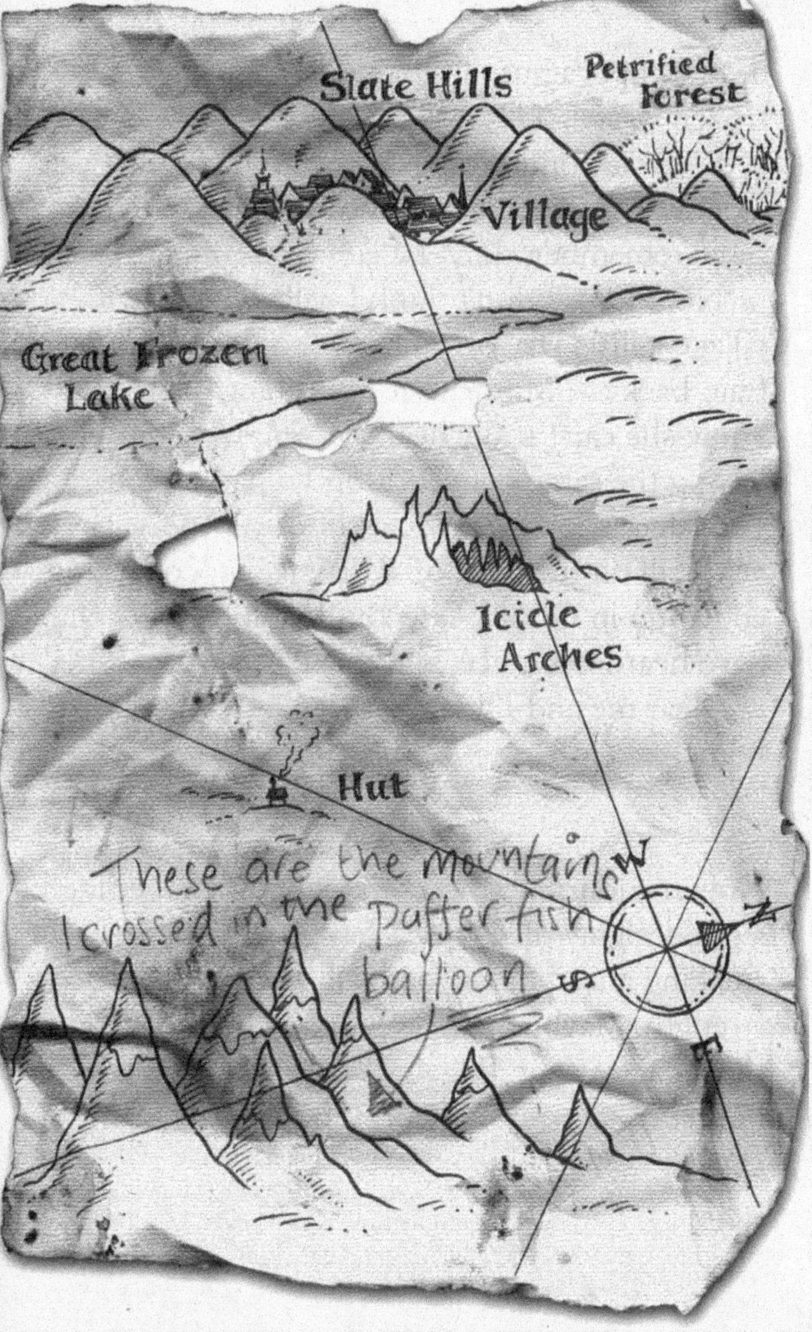

Slate Hills

Petrified Forest

Village

Great Frozen Lake

Icicle Arches

Hut

These are the mountains I crossed in the Puffer fish balloon

W

N

S

dead trapper's hut in the middle of a huge frozen wasteland.'

'Sounds wonderful, dear,' Mum said. 'Oh, wait a minute, Charlie. Here's your dad just come in. Now remember, don't be late for tea . . .'

'No, Mum, I don't think I will. There's a village a little way off and I'm hoping to get a train back . . . Mum?' But Mum rang off. Well, I know she can't really hear me. She was still having the same conversation I'd had with her years ago; soon after I had shot over the waterfall on the back of a massive crocodile and ended up in Gorilla City. But it still feels good to have heard her voice, and one day, perhaps, she *will* hear me and I'll know that I'm getting nearer home.

Now my journal is up to date. I plan on getting a good night's sleep, for I have a day's heavy trekking ahead of me and will need all my strength. Maybe my next entry will be written in the village . . . or, fingers crossed, on a train home!

The Icicle Arches

By the light of the moon and with a safe distance between the arches and me, I am jotting down my latest adventures. I am absolutely famished; I haven't eaten anything since this morning so I've opened a can of baked beans and am eating them cold out of the tin. Lovely!

The scale of the map must be wrong. It's taken me all day to reach the great Icicle Arches, which are only about halfway to the village. It's going to take me longer than I thought, even though I've been travelling much faster than I ever expected.

In a cupboard I'd found Trapper Blane's toolbox, and behind the hut was a pile of old wood. Inspecting the various scraps of wood, I chose a long, narrow plank that had been warped by the wet snow so that one end curved upwards. I was able to plane and sand and polish the plank until it was as smooth as glass. Then with some other scraps of wood, I screwed one piece at right angles to the plank, about three quarters of the way along, and to that I fixed some handles that I had unbolted from a couple of large saucepans. In no time at all I had made myself a snow scooter. This is what it looked like:

Panhandles.

My super-speedy snow scooter!

Warped and polished plank

My rucksack was bulging with fresh supplies. I took some tins of food, the box of matches, a screwdriver, an old transistor radio, some new pencils, a large magnifying glass and a vicious-looking spring-trap that I thought might come in useful one day. With my old clothes stuffed at the bottom of my bag, I pulled on the hunter's heavy fur coat and a spare hat that I found hanging on a hook. With a last look around the cabin, I touched a lighted match to a pile of rags, closed the door and pushed off on my snow scooter.

It worked! The plank slid effortlessly over the snow and I was soon whipping along at a fair old lick. Behind me the burning hut sent a column of smoke curling up into the wide sky. In front of me the fresh, white snow stretched forward to the horizon. It felt good to be travelling again and I scooted to the top of one snow dune, careered down the other side and up to the top of the next.

I was soon eating up the miles, but the sun was already starting to set when I saw the huge arches of ice, looming ahead of me.

Icicles... And Other Things!

A few small columns of ice started to appear; they grew taller and more numerous as I continued to scoot along. Soon these angular columns of ice were all around me, climbing twenty metres into the sky like the pillars of some huge ice cathedral. Then, as the sun touched the horizon and its red fire bled across the landscape, I scooted round a massive pillar and saw the Icicle Arches ahead of me.

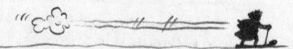

They were magnificent; three huge arcs of blue ice, with rainbow colours flashing along their sides where they were caught by the setting sun. A mass of icicles, ten metres long, hung under the archways, glinting and pulsing with light as if they were alive. I dropped my scooter and ran under one of the arches. Its high, sloping roof sparkled and glittered like a fairytale grotto, curving towards the ground to form an enormous icy cavern. It would be a wonderful shelter for the night!

This is me↗ standing in front of the icicle arch.

I walked further into the arcade of ice, amazed at the beautiful and colourful shapes all around me. All of a sudden I got a terrible tickle at the back of my throat, making my eyes water. I doubled over, racked by a coughing fit, and the sound echoed through the arch. Then, a strange noise came from above, as if a pile of leaves had been disturbed by the wind. I looked around to see if there was anyone there; I couldn't see anything amid the great ice stalactites, but then I heard the rustling noise again.

'Hello?' I called softly. Then louder, 'Is there anybody there?' My voice echoed up to the roof, and the icicles started to shake and rattle like glasses on a tray. I looked up just as one massive shard cracked and fell away from the ceiling. Whoa! I tried to leap out of the way as it fell like a glass javelin towards the ground.

Crash! I wasn't fast enough and the icicle pierced my big fur coat, knocking me down and pinning me to the ground. Just then the roof of the arch filled with a noise like a thousand umbrellas being opened and closed again and again, and as I looked up, a flock of blood-sucking bats

swooped down towards me.

'Help! I screamed, pulling the thick fur collar of my coat up around my ears.

Bat Attack!

They came like a squadron of fighter planes, their leathery wings flapping and their high-pitched squeals splitting the air. *Eeep, Eeep, Eeep!*

The bats flew straight at me like kamikaze pilots, battering me and knocking me this way and that. I tried to pull the icicle out of the ground but it was stuck fast and I was trapped, a human sacrifice to a bunch of blood-guzzling flying rats! I covered my head as the vicious animals streamed over me, taking small chunks out of the backs of my hands with their needle-like fangs.

'Yeagh!' I cried, flailing my arms around wildly; but still they came, in a never-ending barrage. What could I do? How could I stop them? Think, Charlie, I said to myself, *think!* But it isn't easy to think when your head is lost in a cloud of battering, biting bats.

Then I suddenly remembered: bats find their way by sonar. Their high-pitched squeals bounce off any surrounding objects and they can lock in on their prey with the accuracy of a radar-guided missile. I knew just how to upset their radar!

I shrugged off my rucksack as fast as I could and pulled it underneath me. The bats continued to attack, dive-bombing and hitting me with sickening thuds. They screamed and squealed, ripping mouthfuls of fur from my coat and peppering my back with bruises. Then, retreating under my hunter's coat as far as possible, I hunched over the rucksack and scrabbled around inside, pulling out one thing after another. Finally, my hands found Trapper Blane's old radio. I extended the aerial, turned the volume up full and then, twisting the tuning dial back and forth, made the radio squeal and scream.

The strident noises echoed around the arch, making my ears buzz with pain. I just hoped it would have the same effect on the bats!

OOOEEEOoo!

Almost immediately the animals became confused. Their sonar jammed and they began to career into each other, crashing at full speed into the cavern walls. I turned the screeching dial and the flock of bats rose into the air, smashing their way amongst the icicles, which snapped and dropped like a shower of daggers. I remained crouched on the floor as the shards thudded into the ground all around me. *Clink, thud, clink, clang!* Gradually, everything became quiet and I cautiously lifted my head and looked around at the devastation.

Everywhere, huge icy stalactites had pierced the ground, each one stabbing a rampaging bat clean through the middle. I felt sorry for the beasts, but then, remembering how they had swarmed down from the roof to attack me, and looking down at my bleeding hands, I quickly changed my mind. I turned my squawking radio off and, slipping out of my fur coat, which was still pinned to the ground, I got shakily to my feet.

I had never seen bats like this before and in true explorer style I have decided to name this undiscovered species.

The Barbarous Icicle Bat

A large, grey bat the size of a rabbit, with a span of leathery wings about one-and-a-half metres across. They have needle-like fangs, three centimetres long. When hanging from the roof of the cave, with their large, pale wings folded around them, they look just like icicles, becoming perfectly camouflaged in the roof of an ice cave. They are aggressive flesh eaters and attack *en masse,* thousands at a time, giving their prey little chance of escape. They have the scariest faces I've ever seen since starting out on my adventures.

Scooting Through The Night

Having defeated the barbarous bats, I took a flying kick at the vicious-looking icicle that still speared my coat to the floor. I managed to snap the icicle off at the base, and I quickly put my thick fur coat back on. My teeth were chattering like castanets with the cold, but I soon started to warm up again.

I had no desire to hang around the arch any longer than I had to. There might have been another squadron of bats hanging somewhere up in the roof, ready to attack; so I quickly gathered my stuff, threw my rucksack over my back and ran into the night.

On my way out, I noticed a pile of small bones amongst some of the stalagmites. Crouching down, I saw that it was a sort of bat graveyard, and picking up a long fanged skull, I popped it into my rucksack. What better

evidence of my encounter with these disgusting

beasts could I find? My friends at home will be really impressed!

Now, it's time to leave here. I've got a map, my compass and a torch, so I'm going to continue my journey through the night. Retrieving my scooter and checking my compass, I am ready to skate out into the unknown once again.

The sky is alive with twinkling stars from one horizon to the other. Meteors rip across the velvety blackness, trailing tails of yellow fire, and a fat, waxy moon is floating high above me. Let's go!

Shifting Snows

This is amazing! You'll never guess where I am now. The most remarkable thing happened, and *just in the nick of time,* or my journey would already be over. I am aboard an incredible… No, first I must explain how I got here!

I had raced on through the night, leaving the glow of the icicle arches far behind. The moon lit up the ground in front of me as I tirelessly followed my compass west towards the village and civilization. I ignored the strange noises emanating from the shadows either side of me and closed my eyes to the frightful, flapping silhouettes that occasionally flew across the moon; but when I saw the ground ahead of me move and buckle and bulge, I turned my scooter into a skid and came to an abrupt halt.

What was it? Maybe it was the start of an earthquake and the ground would open up in front of me. I watched, fascinated, as the snow rose and fell, billowing like a huge sheet in the wind. Then the snow started to break up, and just below the surface I saw the smooth back of an animal coil forward. Everywhere the snow

43

was collapsing and suddenly one, two, three, no! . . . A hundred stubby heads reared up and sniffed the wind.

They were worms – massive pale pink worms about eight metres long – and they stopped and tested the air with their noses. The one nearest to me lowered his big blunt head and gently nudged my stomach. I held my breath, remaining perfectly still as it bumped and prodded, sniffing away like a huge short-sighted vacuum cleaner hose.

Saved By My Pyjamas

Glancing around, I noticed that the other worms were starting to slowly but surely make their way towards me. In another few minutes I would be surrounded. If I had been quicker, and made a break for it then, I might have made it. But I hesitated and soon the worms were advancing in too great a number to dodge. I was being encircled by a solid wall of worms! What could I do?

The nearest worm sniffed and nudged me again. As he tried to focus with his tiny little eyes, I realized the worms relied more on their sense of smell than on their poor eyesight. I stepped back, and for a second the worm lost me. His head swayed to the left and right, sniffing at the air. But then he caught my whiff again and started forwards.

I took another few steps back, my hand searching through my trusty explorer's kit. If it was something whiffy they wanted, then I had just the thing! I found my tatty, pongy pyjamas and pulled them out. Stepping as far away from the nearest worm as possible without getting too close to the others, I kneeled down in the snow. The worms were closing in from all directions.

I started to push and pile the snow up and in double-quick time I made a very rough snowman, about the same size as me. As the worms ploughed closer and closer, I dressed the snow-Charlie in my pyjamas. I'd been wearing them at bedtime ever since my journey started and they were now more than a little smelly.

Immediately, the worms caught the ripe scent of my pyjamas, and their noses wrinkled in excitement. They slid forwards as quickly as their huge bulks would allow, and I flattened myself down in the snow. The worms crowded around my decoy and attacked. Luckily they were soon in a ferocious feeding frenzy and I could push my way out between two of the big, blubbery bits of fish bait without being noticed.

Using their great blunt heads as battering rams, the worms pounded the snowman flat. Picking up the pyjamas in their toothless but powerful jaws, they pulled and squabbled and

The worms attacked
my snowman!

tore the material to shreds. As soon as I had
crawled clear of them, I shakily and silently
crept over to my scooter. With a final look
behind me at the battling snow worms, I
scooted off as fast as I could go. Fantastic, I
thought; saved by a pair of smelly pyjamas!

As the sun rose the following morning, I
reached the top of a low hill and found myself
looking across a great, frozen lake; a lake as
wide and empty as an ocean. In the far distance
I could see a faint blue smudge that was the

Slate Hills. I knew that somewhere, nestled in a valley amongst those hills, was the village. I scooted out onto the ice. Nothing could stop me now.

Well, I should have known better, because I had only gone a fraction of the way when all my plans collapsed from under my feet!

A Huge Swallow

My scooter whizzed across the hard, shiny ice at super-speed, and I whooped with delight. At this speed I might reach the Slate Hills by suppertime. Maybe I would find a burger bar there and treat myself to a quarterpounder and fries; I'm sure I still had a few doubloons in my pocket! I could look for the railway station and, with any luck, be on a train home by tomorrow morning.

Then, all of a sudden, my scooter started to slow as it sent a shower of slush shooting out behind. Looking down, I noticed there was a film of water lying on the surface of the ice. What was happening?

The scooter slowed some more, and as the slush grew deeper and deeper, it became harder and harder to push along.

'Drat!' I yelled. At this rate it would be quicker to walk; but when I stepped onto the ice, I disappeared up to my knees in thick, gunky slush. Worse still, if I stood in one place too long, my boots started to sink even further, and I was in danger of falling right through the quagmire of half-melted ice into the chilly waters below.

I pulled first one boot and then the other out of the gunge, but as soon as I put them down, they were swallowed up in the frozen morass and I started to sink once again. I threw myself onto my tummy on the ground, spreading out my arms and legs to increase my surface area. It  worked – I was no longer sinking; but I wasn't going anywhere either!

I tried a sort of breaststroke action and found I could propel myself along, but at this rate it would take a year and a day to reach the Slate Hills. Perhaps I should go back the way I had come? No! After all this effort and coming all this way and knowing that a village of people lay just over the horizon, I couldn't turn round now. What should I do?

As I lay there with the tip of my nose touching the icy water, thinking over my dilemma, I suddenly saw a huge shadow pass under me, deep beneath the ice. What on earth was that? My heart flipped as the shadow passed beneath me once again. I started to paddle quickly, trying to reach solid ground where I could stand up and run.

It ploughed through the ice!

'Quickly,' I cried, urging myself on, 'there's something down there!' I flapped about on the ice like an overgrown turtle until, eventually, I felt firmer ice beneath me so I could pull myself up onto one knee. Just then, the ice behind me exploded into a million shards. I span round, and there, about a hundred metres away, and travelling as fast as an intercity express train, was the largest mouth I had ever seen; and there was no doubt about it – the gaping maw was coming straight for me!

I tried to escape, but I didn't stand a chance.

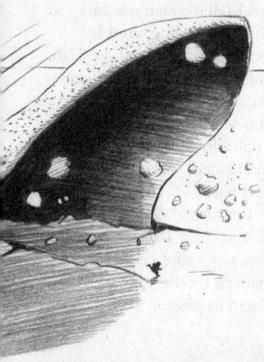 The monster ploughed through the ice after me, and as its huge jaw towered above my head, the ice beneath my feet gave way. I dropped into the freezing waters, gasping at the sudden

cold and sinking into the icy depths below.

Then my world exploded in a torrent of bubbles and great bucketfuls of ice showered down on me as the mighty jaws of the sea creature closed over my head, and I was swallowed up by darkness.

In The Beast's Belly

'HELP!' I cried. The gigantic sea creature had swallowed me, and I fell through the dark, rolling and tumbling and yelling, until I bounced on something soft and spongy. Ugh, disgusting! Was this its tongue? I kicked and fought, hoping the monster would spit me out before I was swallowed into its stomach, but to no avail; I rolled right down the back of the animal's throat and landed, soaking wet, with a clang on something hard.

That was odd! I crouched down and had a good feel around. Yes, there was no doubt about it, the floor was metal; I could feel a raised diamond pattern on the panels and the rivets that fixed them in place.

All of a sudden a light glowed bright and I could see that I was in a sort of metal box. What sort of creature was this? On one side was a door with a large wheel on it. The wheel turned easily and the heavy door swung open, revealing a long dark passage. This was no animal – it was some sort of craft. I had been swallowed by a monstrous submarine!

On one side was a door

A row of wall lights came on in the passage and I followed them, past rooms full of roaring machinery, until I came to another door. It opened onto a brightly-lit room as large as an aircraft hangar, where gleaming steel blocks towered above me like skyscrapers. There was no one around, so I hurried across the room until I came to the foot of a ladder and started to climb.

This is me!
↓

I hurried across the room . . .

Is Anybody There?

Pulling myself through an open hatchway, I stepped onto an empty landing. Another climb took me to the next level, and this too was deserted. Where was everybody? The submarine was as empty as the *Mary Celeste*.

'Is there anybody there?' I yelled, but there was no reply. I was feeling very uneasy now; if the ship was crewed, then where were the people? Were they alive? Were they friends or foe? If the ship was deserted, then how on earth was I going to get off and continue my journey home?

I crept along a passage to another door and as I opened it, I was met by one of the most incredible sights of my travels so far.

Under The Ice In The Hydro - Electric Whale

For a scary moment I thought I had stepped out of the submarine and into the water, as there were strange, brilliantly-coloured fish swimming all around me. Then I realized I was under a huge glass dome, ringed with searchlights that illuminated the underwater world outside.

Here are some of the amazing fish I saw swimming outside.

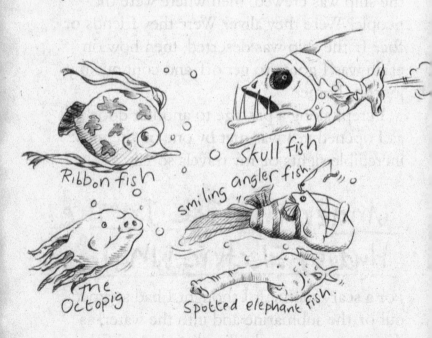

Ribbon fish

Skull fish

smiling angler fish

The Octopig

Spotted elephant fish

Gradually, the searchlights outside dimmed and, like a rising sun, the lights inside the glass dome came on. I was in a large observation lounge, arranged with comfortable sofas and low, fin-shaped tables. On one of the tables was a pile of leaflets and, picking one up to read, I finally discovered where I was. The leaflet explained it all:

I'll stick it into the next page so you can see how amazing it looked!

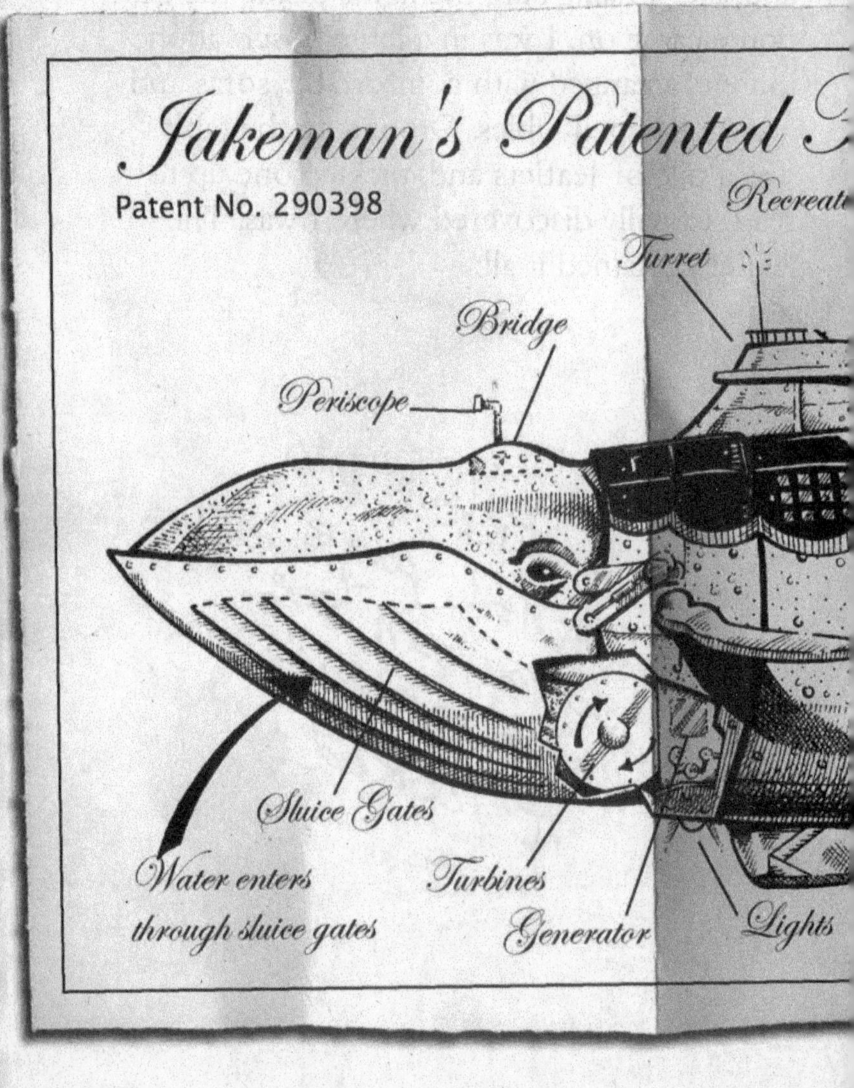

Jakeman's Patented

Patent No. 290398

Recreate

Turret

Bridge

Periscope

Sluice Gates

Water enters through sluice gates

Turbines

Generator

Lights

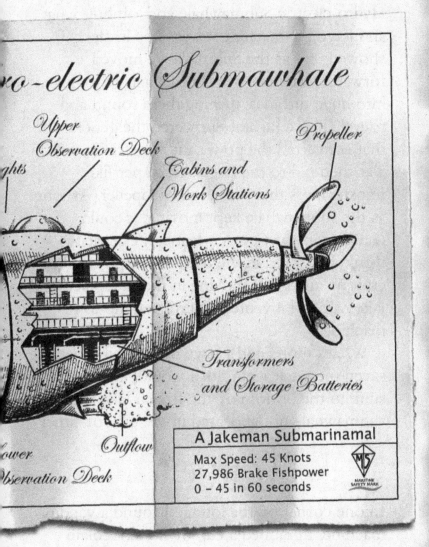

...ro-electric *Submawhale*

Upper
Observation Deck

...ghts

Cabins and
Work Stations

Propeller

Transformers
and Storage Batteries

...ower

Outflow

Observation Deck

A Jakeman Submarinamal

Max Speed: 45 Knots
27,986 Brake Fishpower
0 – 45 in 60 seconds

MS
MARITIME
SAFETY MARK

As you can see, I was aboard a Jakeman's Hydro-electric Submawhale and, oh boy, what an incredible machine it was! The leaflet showed that as the Submawhale moved forward, water was forced through sluice gates into huge turbines, turning them round and round. These turbines powered the generators that converted the power into electricity, which was then fed to the huge skyscraper-like transformers that turned the propeller. As long as the submawhale kept moving, it could generate its own power. Enough electricity would be stored in the batteries to power the craft up and get it moving in the first place. Jakeman had invented a perpetual motion machine!

What's more, and I have no idea why, he had saved me once again, for I would have surely sunk to the bottom of the frozen lake had the submawhale not appeared in the nick of time!

Trapped

In one corner of the lounge I found a vending machine. I grabbed a cup of hot chocolate (and, oh boy, was it delicious!) and then sat down at one of the tables to write up my latest adventures. And here I am!

I don't feel so spooked now that I know I am aboard a Jakeman machine. Although I have no idea who he is, his inventions have always proved good allies. It's still creepy, though, knowing that there is no one on board . . . but hold on a minute! There has to be a pilot on board, doesn't there? Otherwise, who's driving this monstrous submathingy?

A tannoy has just popped into life, nearly scaring me out of my wits, and a booming voice echoed through the sub: 'The Submawhale has crossed the frozen lake and we are now travelling at a depth of five fathoms, through tiny passages beneath the Slate Hills. The Submawhale has crossed the frozen lake and we are now travelling at a depth . . . '

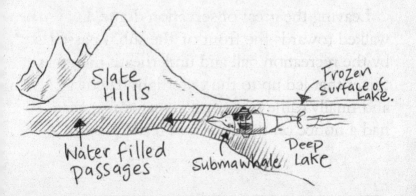

Oh no! This is a disaster. If the whale has just cruised beneath the landmass, then how on earth am I ever going to get back up top? Apart from the frozen lake, there is nowhere we could surface. I have to talk to the pilot, pronto. Who knows, it might even be Jakeman himself!

I'll write more when I've spoken him.

I'm having a 🚂 of a time!

The Pressure ~~Bf~~ Builds

Well, things didn't work out quite as I expected, but I'm not complaining! For the first time since leaving home, I am sitting up in a proper bed with proper sheets. A steaming mug of cocoa and a plate of biscuits stand on the bedside table as I write down the strange turn of events that brought me here.

Leaving the great observation dome, I walked towards the front of the sub. I passed by the recreation hall and underneath the great turret that led up to the watertight hatchway, and finally came to a small antechamber that had a notice on the door that read *Pressure*

Control Room. I stepped inside and heard the door lock behind me.

Whoa! What had the door locked for? Starting to panic, I yanked at the handle but it wouldn't budge. I turned to the door in the opposite wall of the chamber. A small sign stated quite clearly:

Bridge. Captain W. Jakeman.
KNOCK AND WAIT.

I breathed a sigh of relief. It *was* Jakeman and I was sure I had no reason to worry. I knocked and waited.

There was no reply, so I knocked again and waited again. Still there was no reply, so I tried the handle and found to my horror that this door was locked as well. As a loud hiss escaped from some pipes that ran around the floor, I started to lose my nerve and thumped on the door with all my might.

'Mr Jakeman, let me in, I need to talk to you. Mr Jakeman,' I yelled, but my voice was drowned out as the hissing from the pipes grew louder. My ears started to ache and pop as the air pressure inside the chamber grew. I was just beginning to wonder if I was going to be squashed as flat as a board, when there was a great rushing sound, and I shot straight up, through a vent in the ceiling. and along a wide corrugated pipe. With a huge belch of air and an explosion of bubbles, I was ejected into the water.

Hubble And Bubble And Here Comes Trouble!

Silver bubbles boiled all around me. I held my breath, waiting to feel the chill of the freezing waters . . . but it never came. I realized that I wasn't wet at all, and finally, letting my breath out in a rush, discovered that I could breathe quite easily. How was that possible? I was under water, but I could breathe!

Reaching out a hand, I touched a silvery wall of water that curved over my head, around my sides and under my feet. I was standing inside a giant bubble, rising rapidly through the jet-black sea! Looking up, I noticed a tiny circle of light, like a full moon, which grew and grew as I raced up through the sea in my pressurized bubble.

I was heading straight for it, and as the circle of light grew to the size of a fairground roundabout, I surfaced and the bubble popped. I found myself floundering in the bottom of a stone fountain, water spraying from the mouth of a carved fish that looked remarkably like the submawhale. Swimming to the edge of the fountain, I clambered onto the low wall and sat down.

This was incredible! I had surfaced in a fountain pool, in the middle of a cobbled market square, in a village that looked like something out of a fairytale. Houses with steep pitched roofs crowded in on each other, leaning at crazy angles over dark, narrow alleyways.

The market square was a hive of activity. Villagers were busy shaking rugs from their windows, sweeping the cobbles outside their shops, or standing in doorways chatting to their neighbours. It was late evening and the market traders were busy putting up their stalls for tomorrow's market, erecting long trestle tables and unfurling brightly-coloured canvas awnings.

Jakeman had done it again; I was sure he had delivered me to the heart of the village marked on Trapper Blane's map! I was dripping wet, but surely I was among friends at last.

A Warning!

Still in a bit of a daze, I wandered aimlessly through the square. I felt so happy to be among people again after my lonely flight across the Pangaean Ocean and my dangerous travels through the frozen wastelands.

I was still in a bit of a daze!

This is what the market square looked like.

(sort of!)

'Hello,' I babbled as I passed through the crowd. 'Good evening, my name is Charlie Small and I'm trying to get back home. Is there a railway sta—?' I stopped talking, for when the market traders saw me their jaws dropped and they started to run towards me, their faces etched with fear and panic.

'What . . . what's the matter?' I cried as they pushed me, gesticulating wildly with their hands. I knew I must look a dreadful sight in my filthy and soaking animal-skin clothes, but this reaction seemed a bit strong! A man with a dark, curly beard stepped forward and pointed, way beyond the Slate Hills. His lips were moving but I couldn't hear a word, because my ears were still fuzzy from the pressure chamber.

I banged and shook my head, trying to make my ears pop, but it was no good. I could only hear vague, muffled voices. I backed into a doorway in the corner of the square. I had no idea what was going on and I was becoming more than a little scared. In a desperate attempt to hear what was being said, I held my nose, clamped my mouth tight shut and blew. POP! At last! My ears popped and the sudden noise of the clamouring crowd sounded very loud.

'Are you mad?' the bearded man was saying fiercely, pointing to a poster pasted on the wall. 'He'll be here tomorrow. Go while you still have a chance.'

'Yes, get out while you can,' agreed the crowd. 'Before tomorrow morning!'

'You've been warned,' said the man, grabbing my arm.

'Warned about what?' I asked, but again the man just pointed to the poster. 'Just don't be around when the show comes to town!'

With that, the crowd turned as one and hurried back to their stalls. Shooting the occasional worried glance in my direction and muttering amongst themselves, they carried on with their chores. Well! I thought. Not exactly the sort of welcome I was hoping for!

Intrigued, I studied the poster.

FOR ONE DAY ONLY AND FOR YOUR DELIGHT

THE PUPPET MASTER

RETURNS TO REPEAT HIS WORLD FAMOUS
FEATS OF PUPPETEERING PERFECTION

HERE ON MARKET DAY
ALL VILLAGERS WILL ATTEND
PRICE: ONE

Well! I thought again. What a lot of fuss about nothing! I quite liked puppet shows. This one must be *really* bad for the villagers to get so worked up! The poster seemed a little bossy, demanding that all the villagers must attend the performance; but if the puppeteer was as bad as his critics made out, maybe that was the only way he could get people to come – to make them feel like they had no choice! Anyway, I thought it sounded as if it might be fun.

The poster was smudged where the price was printed, and as I leaned forwards to have a closer look, a small, bony hand suddenly grabbed my shoulder and I was pulled into the doorway behind me. The door slammed shut and I found myself in complete darkness.

I See The Light

Whoever it was scrabbled around in the dark. Then there was the scrape of a match, a bloom of light and I stared into the pale, watery eyes of probably the oldest woman in the world! She was a tiny little thing, as thin as a chicken's leg, and bowed at the shoulder like a walking stick. Her hands fluttered in the air like startled birds, but

73

her wrinkled lips were set firm and her pointed chin was thrust forward confidently.

We were standing in an ironmonger's shop surrounded by lead piping, copper tubes, valves, sprockets and gaskets. The walls were lined with blackened wood and brass-handled drawers. Lanterns hung from every available space on the ceiling, and buckets and tools of every description filled the floor. It was an Aladdin's cave of bric-a-brac!

The old woman wore a bell-shaped hat pulled low over her forehead, and a dark astrakhan coat buttoned up to her neck that somehow gave her the appearance of an ancient gnome from a fairy-tale. She put her finger to her lips and beckoned me to follow her. We went down a passage that led from the back of the shop into the kitchen, where a bench was drawn close to the range.

'You can stay here tonight, my dear, but you must leave this place before first light,' said the old woman, in a surprisingly clear and musical voice. 'You are not safe. No indeed, not in the least bit safe.'

'Everybody keeps telling me that,' I said. 'What's going on?'

'The Puppet Master is coming,' she cried,
wringing her hands.

'Everybody in the town keeps telling me that as well,' I said. 'I'm not afraid of a silly puppeteer!'

But the old woman grabbed my shoulders and put her face close to mine. 'This one is different,' she whispered. 'Oh yes indeed, this one is very different! He comes to perform his show once, sometimes twice a year. We're never sure when until his posters appear overnight, but every time he brings his show he demands a child in payment.'

A child! So that's what the poster had said, and then it struck me – I hadn't seen a single child outside in the busy market square. There were no children anywhere! I didn't like the sound of this at all. Perhaps I should leave the village before the Puppet Master arrived.

'Is there a railway station in the town?' I asked.

'No, dear,' said the old lady. 'There's nothing like that here, I'm afraid.'

'Darn it,' I sighed. 'Never mind, I will just have to keep on walking. Don't worry; I will go before the puppet show comes to town.' For the first time the old lady smiled and it lit up the whole room, and with it the mood of danger was lifted too.

'Good, now let's get you dry and have some supper,' she said.

A Terrible Bedtime Tale

The old woman cooked me a meal while I dried my clothes in front of the range, and as she cooked she talked. She told me all about the puppeteer and how, when he first arrived, he had been welcomed by the villagers.

It wasn't often that any form of entertainment found its way to the sleepy little village amongst the hills, and the villagers had enjoyed his performances and paid him handsomely. He was certainly a very gifted puppeteer and seemed to make the marionettes leap and dance at will. It wasn't until later that night, after the Puppet Master had packed up and gone, that someone noticed one of the village children was missing.

A search party was organized and they travelled far into the hills, calling and calling until their voices were hoarse. There had been a heavy fall of snow that day, and on one of the hillside paths the search party discovered that there had been an avalanche. Rocks and trees had been

77

swept down into an inaccessible ravine. Everyone knew the boy had an adventurous spirit and loved to go exploring through the hills. At last it was assumed that he had gone out walking, perhaps following the Puppet Master's caravan, and been swept over the edge and to the bottom of the ravine below.

The old woman finished at the stove and dished up the best meal I'd had since leaving home: thick slices of bacon, a rich yellow egg, baked beans and a mountain of crispy chips. I tucked in, but ate in silence as she continued with her story.

Bacon and eggs are great!

The Village Learns The Truth

'The town mourned the loss of the boy in what was seen as a tragic accident, but gradually, over time, life started to return to normal. It wasn't until one year later, when the Puppet Master reappeared in his brightly coloured caravan, that everyone realized what had really happened.

'At the show that night, the puppets swirled and twisted and danced to the music from an old steam-driven organ on the back of the puppeteer's van. We were completely caught up in the magic of the show, and laughed and cheered for the first time since the boy's disappearance; but when the Puppet Master reached behind him and brought another puppet into the routine, the whole crowd gasped in astonishment. For it was obvious to all of us, despite his fixed expression and stiff little limbs, that the puppet was the very boy who had gone missing. Somehow, by magic or science, or just plain wickedness, the Puppet Master had turned that child into a dumb, staring and helpless puppet.'

The Puppet Master Speaks

Here the old woman took a grubby handkerchief from her pocket, lifted her glasses and dabbed at her watery eyes. Then, taking a deep breath, she continued.

'The crowd roared in anger, bringing the show to a stop, and we demanded the return of the lost child. The Puppet Master simply folded his arms and stared at us from under his bushy brow until, gradually, the noise died to a terrible silence. Yes indeed, such a terrible silence! Finally he spoke, with a voice so warm and syrupy that we became hypnotized.

' "Oh dear me," he said. "How terribly ungrateful you are! After I have entertained you with skills that you could never have imagined, you accuse me of stealing one worthless boy. Well, I didn't steal him. He ran after me, begging to join my unique travelling extravaganza. How could I say no? All little boys want to run away and join the circus and all I have done is to make his wish come true. Now you're asking me to break his little wooden heart and turn him away?

' "No, the boy stays with me, and the price

for tonight's show is another child and the next time I return, you will give me another. How else shall I get my magical marionettes without the generous donations from such friendly villages as yours? How else can I continue to delight my audiences across the land?"

'With that, the Puppet Master leaped onto the front of his caravan and flicked the reins, sending his horse clattering out of the square. "See you next time," he called with an evil cackle.

"Ha ha ha!" — evil cackle

The Old Lady's Granddaughter

'We were all still sitting around in a trance, but gradually we regained our senses. We vowed that the Puppet Master would never take another of our children, and that night we locked all our doors and windows and the menfolk patrolled the square. Nobody saw a thing, but when the sun rose the next morning, another child had gone, taken as if by magic. Many more children have disappeared since, and if we were to try and stand up to him, we'd never see them again. A year ago he took my precious granddaughter. She's all I have in the world, but now the only chance I get to see her is when the Puppet Master comes here.'

The poor old woman burst into tears and I put my arm around her skinny shoulders. 'It's a dreadful story,' I said. 'I don't know what to say. Is there anything I can do to help?'

'Just keep your promise and leave the village before sunrise tomorrow,' she wept. 'Get out before the Puppet Master comes!'

Sweet Dreams

The old woman, who insisted I call her Granny Green, showed me to a guest room, leaving a mug of cocoa and a plate of biscuits on the bedside table. As I crawled into the first proper bed I had seen since leaving home, Granny Green wished me goodnight.

She pulled a slab of toffee, with a little toffee hammer, from her apron pocket. 'I don't suppose you've had much in the way of sweets recently,' she smiled. 'This used to be my granddaughter's favourite,' and she tucked it under my pillow. I thanked her, and then,

although I was
feeling exhausted, I
dragged the journal
out of my rucksack. I
wanted to write down my
adventures while they were still
fresh in my memory.

The toffee hammer.

It's been an action-packed few days, that's for
sure. And what about the dreadful story that the
old woman has just told me. Is it true? The
Puppet Master sounds like something out of a
horror story; but I know, real or not, I am not
going to risk bumping into him. I'll grab a few
hours' sleep, then leave this sad and troubled
place far behind me. I have got some travelling
to do and can't wait to get started on my journey
again.

Goodnight. I will write more as soon as I can.

Help Me

No!

What's going on?

Where am I?

Get Lost

oh NO!!

Who are you?

I can't move

Much Later

It has been some time since I last had the chance to write up my journal and I would really rather not relive my latest adventure. It is probably the darkest and scariest part of my travels so far; but this is supposed to be a record of all my escapades, so I will grit my teeth and continue . . .

After I'd finished writing up my latest adventures, I lay back on the comfortable pillow in Granny Green's guest room. I pulled the duvet up under my chin and yawned. I was so tired and my head began to swim with thoughts of home. I imagined Mum and Dad busy downstairs, as I pretended to lie in my very own bed in my very own bedroom.

Suddenly I felt a long, long way from home, and even though I knew how the conversation would go, I wanted to hear my mum's voice again. Fighting sleep, I fished around in my rucksack for my mobile phone and charger. I span the charger's handle, dialled my home number, put the phone to my ear and promptly fell fast asleep . . .

Sleepwalking Into Disaster!

Dreams of home swirled through my head, mixed up with images of gorillas and pirates and my old enemy, Joseph Craik. Then I could hear my mum calling, 'Char-lie! Wake up, Charlie.'

'Just a few more minutes, Mum,' I mumbled. Surely it wasn't school time already! I was so tired I felt I could sleep for a week, but Mum's voice continued.

'Come on, Charlie, it's time to get up. Char-lie!' My eyes popped open, expecting to see Mum standing with her arms folded at the foot of my bed, but instead I saw a strange room flooded with moonlight.

Where am I? I wondered. I sat up, my mobile falling onto the pillow, and looked around the unfamiliar room. Then I remembered: I was in the guest room of the old lady's shop. I felt under the pillow and found the slab of toffee she had given me.

I must have dreamed I could hear my mum calling me. But all of a sudden, I heard the familiar voice again!

'Char-lie! Come on, Charlie, get up.'

I looked around in a panic, but there was nobody there. Where was it coming from?

My mobile – the voice was coming from my mobile! I scrabbled around in my bed, picked it up and put it to my ear.

'Mum?' I said frantically. 'Is that you?'

'Come on, Charlie, it's time to get up,' said her voice. I found myself getting dressed in my old clothes, stuffing the toffee and little hammer into my pocket and creeping quietly over to the bedroom door.

Answering The Call

Mum's voice no longer seemed to come from my phone, but from somewhere outside.

I lifted the latch and crept downstairs. Making sure the little shop bell didn't ring, I opened the front door and stepped out into the now deserted market place.

In a dreamlike state, I followed the sound across the square and down a dark, dank alley.

Charlie

I walked between rows of sleeping houses and right out of the town. Over hills and across valleys, I followed Mum's voice as it called me on. Then, as I crossed the brow

Charlie

of another hill, her voice was joined by the sound of the most delicate music.

In The Petrified Forest

It sounded like the tootling of panpipes, and as I walked on, the music became louder, an orchestra of flutes filling the air. I turned a bend in the road and found myself looking down at a forest of strange and decayed beauty. I learned later that it was the Petrified Forest

Trapper Blane had marked on his map, a forest of dead and fossilized trees.

As I walked through the forest, I heard the music coming from the trees themselves. Their trunks had become hollow and, as the wind passed through the holes, they acted like huge organ pipes, each tree producing a different note.

Now, as the air around me gently shifted, a chorus of notes filled the air, like the cries of singing whales. Woven into the wonderful, airborne melody was the voice . . . Mum's voice. Although it didn't sound *quite* so much like my mum's voice any more.

I walked between two great gnarled tree trunks and stepped out into a clearing, where I saw a dark shape, silhouetted against the light of a campfire. A cloaked figure sat with its back to me, hunched over the embers of a fire. Was it really my mother? I crept forward.

'Mum?' I whispered.

'Charlie,' said the figure turning around. 'We've been waiting for you.'

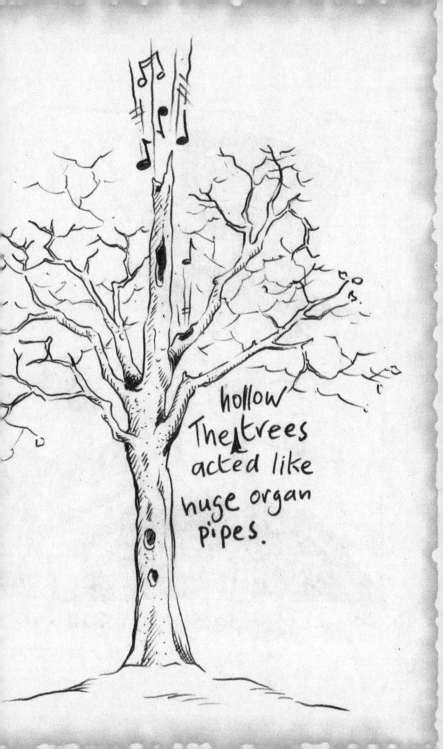

The hollow trees acted like huge organ pipes.

The Puppet Master.

I stepped back. Oh, I wished I had stayed in bed at the shop! I wished I'd stayed at home. I wished I were a million miles from that clearing in the rotted forest, for, as the sky turned opal white and a new day dawned, I could see a man's face; his grey skin and large hooked nose, his fat dry lips and empty black eyes. Behind him I saw the legend painted on the side of his caravan:

INCREDIBLE, WONDERFUL,
AND SOLELY FOR YOUR DELIGHT,

THE PUPPET
MASTER!

A maestro of marionette manipulation!

No! I turned to run, but somehow my feet seemed rooted to the ground.

'Don't go, Charlie,' smiled the Puppet Master. 'I have something for you.' He dipped a mug into the pot that was bubbling over the glowing embers of the fire, filling it with a liquid that steamed in the cold morning air.

The smell was intoxicating. It floated in the air, a visible blue mist that wrapped itself around my head, filling my nostrils. I knew I shouldn't, but I couldn't help myself. I grabbed the mug from his hand and drank the warm, syrupy liquid.

The sweet taste flooded through my body, making my fingers tingle and the breath judder in my chest. The tingling in my fingers increased to a dull throb, making them feel swollen and numb. I looked at my hands and gasped in fear. Tiny crystals were forming on my fingers, multiplying and joining together to form a new outer skin.

The tingling sensations travelled up my arms and across my chest, the new skin forming like a crust as the feeling spread across my body. As the warmth of the liquid cooled in my tummy and the tingling subsided, I could feel the new skin start to harden. Now my face started to grow a second, solid skin. I tried to call out, but my jaw was set as hard as stone. I couldn't believe it! After all the old woman's warnings I was becoming another of the Puppet Master's marionettes. I don't know exactly what had happened, or how it worked. To this day I have no idea what the shell that formed around me was made of. Perhaps it was some sort of plastic, or maybe a very strong ceramic. Whatever it was, it felt as if I had been coated in concrete, or squeezed into a tight-fitting shell, exactly the same shape as my body . . . and I was no longer able to move!

The new skin formed like a crust!

shell → ← skin

A hard shell formed over my skin

I had become a puppet

Taken Alive!

The Puppet Master watched, stony-faced, as I solidified into one of his puppets. Then, as he stood up and stretched, I saw how very tall he was; at least three metres high, and as thin as a whip. He looked like a circus performer on stilts, or an overgrown insect tottering awkwardly on long, spidery legs, waving his thin, willowy arms in the air to keep his balance. He towered over me, and every time he moved his joints crackled like dry leaves.

He picked me up by the scruff of the neck and took me inside his caravan. My eyes opened wide in surprise as I was carried into the crowded interior, for hundreds of other puppets were hanging in long rows from hooks on the ceiling. Like me, they couldn't utter a word and the room was deathly silent. They revolved slowly on the ends of their strings, swinging slightly as the Puppet Master's weight shifted across the caravan. Hundreds of eyes followed us as the Puppet Master carried me over to a small bench in the corner. Here he sorted through lengths of fine string and wooden blocks and, for the first time, I could study his face properly. It is a face I will never forget as long as I live.

The whites of his eyes were a dirty yellow, the irises a dull jet black, and they stared out from under a heavy, beetling brow. The Puppet Master's hooked nose, as craggy as a shard of granite, curved down towards a pointed beard that thrust forward from his chin. But the most disturbing thing about him was that I couldn't hear him breathe, even when he held me close to his face and looked into my eyes. He ran a dry purple tongue along his grey lips in concentration as he tied one end of the twine to my hands and feet, and the other to a cross of wood that he had fashioned from the scraps on the table.

'Welcome to our happy little family, Charlie,' he said in his smooth, silky voice. 'Now I can make you dance and sing to any tune I play . . . and the tune I choose to play the most is fast and loose; fast and loose with other people's money. Hee hee!'

I had no idea what this tall, spidery man was on about, and I stared out angrily at him from behind my shell skin.

'Oh, we have a little rebel, do we?' he smiled, shaking me roughly so my limbs clattered against each other. 'Don't worry, Charlie; you will see what I mean soon enough – and you'd better prove to be a profitable puppet. Otherwise you will end up as just another abandoned toy by the roadside!' Chuckling, he hung me from a spare hook on the ceiling.

Here I swayed, trapped, as the Puppet Master emptied my rucksack onto the workbench and sorted through my explorer stuff.

'What a load of old rubbish!' he exclaimed, finding nothing that interested him. Shoving everything back into the rucksack, he threw it onto a high shelf.

Then the Puppet Master climbed through to the driver's seat, flicked the reins of his horse and we bumped across the clearing along a track leading back through the Petrified Forest and off towards the village.

I flexed my muscles, pushing with all my might against the hard shell that had formed around me, but it was no good. *I couldn't move a finger.* I looked over at the other puppets swinging from the beams, and their scared wide eyes stared back at me.

How on earth was I going to get out of this one?

My Dancing Debut

When the caravan pulled into the same market square I had left only hours before, I could hear the hubbub of nervous voices from the crowd that had already gathered. The Puppet Master threw open the tailgates of his caravan and, like a gigantic pop-up book, a stage unfolded with curtains and placards already in place. He flicked a switch and a wonderful, miniature steam-organ hissed into life, sending music swirling into the air.

'Ladies and gentlemen,' announced the Puppet Master. 'For your delight and amazement, the performance you are about to witness takes the entertainment of puppetry to an art of the highest level, using techniques learned on my travels to the mysterious lands of the east, and with puppets acquired from all corners of the known world.'

'Children, you mean. Not puppets!' a brave person shouted from the rear of the crowd, but the Puppet Master ignored the interruption.

'You will see my puppets dance,' he cried dramatically. 'You will hear them sing. You will see my puppets perform the most amazing feats of magic imaginable!'

With that, there was an explosion of purple smoke, a drum roll sounded and the Puppet Master gathered an armful of puppets, swinging them out onto the stage, already dancing and leaping. They turned and twisted, pirouetted and pranced, child-sized puppets moving as lightly as feathers. In firecracker puffs of smoke, puppets disappeared to be instantly replaced by others, and the show was so good and the spectacle so great that even the crowd of childless villagers forgot themselves and clapped.

Now it was my turn, and I was whisked from my hook and onto the stage. In a blur of lights and faces, my arms and legs were sent into kicks, postures and steps as the Master twitched and pulled and flicked the strings fixed to them. I'd never moved so fast, even when I was escaping from the mandrills near Gorilla City! Pretty soon my head was spinning and I began to feel nauseous.

Then, just as quickly, I was hanging from my hook again. I heaved a sigh of relief; it's a horrible feeling, whizzing around so fast that the whole world is a blur but at the same time not being able move a muscle by yourself. Thank

I was whisked onto the stage!

goodness that's over, I sighed; but no sooner had the thought entered my head than I was off again, sweeping through the air in a majestic leap and back onto the stage!

As the routine went on, the Puppet Master swapped and changed the dancing dolls with the slightest of movements, building to a fantastic finale where he was working a score of puppets at the same time. We careered around the stage, all performing individual kicks and whirls, weaving in and around each other.

It must have been a breathtaking sight, and it's weird, I know, but as we were sent out to take our bows, I felt quite pleased with myself. Not bad for a first show, I stupidly thought, forgetting in the excitement that I'd had nothing to do with it and was just a performing prisoner of the Puppet Master.

As I took my bows, I scanned the audience, expecting to see delight and awe on their faces, but of course I didn't. The whole of the village was clapping as ordered, but staring earnestly as they tried to catch a glimpse of their long-lost children. Now and again a member of the audience would gasp, or call out a name if they recognized anyone.

Then I spotted Granny Green sitting in the audience with a look of horror on her face, and I remembered my desperate situation. When the old lady saw me, tears sprang to her eyes and she pulled herself up from her chair.

'Enough!' she called out to the Puppet Master. 'Haven't you taken enough?'

'Keep quiet, old woman!' hissed the audience. 'Or he won't come back again.'

The old lady collapsed back down in her chair. She knew they were right; if the Puppet Master disappeared for good, they would never see their children again.

A Silent Show

After the show, when all the puppets were back in the caravan and hanging from the ceiling, the townsfolk queued outside. For the right price, money or secrets or promises, they were allowed inside the caravan, to walk past the strange and silent crowd of suspended children.

The kind old lady shuffled past, reaching out to touch my arm. I could feel the warmth of her hand through my hard shell of skin. Then I heard her sob as she recognized her granddaughter, once a pretty girl, now an old

Granny Green's Granddaughter!

and battered doll. The puppet's eyes leaked tears as the old woman went to hug her, but she was forced out of reach by the push of the crowd.

Then all of a sudden the doors were slammed shut, the Puppet Master shooed away the crowd, and with a flick of the reins the caravan rumbled out of the market square, out of the village and into the surrounding countryside.

You won't get away with this, Puppet Master, I thought. *I'll make sure of that, you despicable old despot!*

On Tour With The Puppet Man

Over the following months, we travelled from one end of the valley to the other, giving countless performances to hundreds of villages. I danced on village greens, in busy markets, at inns and in castles. Everywhere we went, a new puppet was added to the Master's collection; and sometimes he would abandon an old puppet by the roadside.

The Puppet Master dazzled his audiences with shows of music and light and movement. He mesmerized them with honeyed words and sleight of hand, mixing his puppet shows with flashes of brilliant magic. With a twist of his wrist and to a clash of his steam-driven cymbals, he would produce a glittering jewel from the mouth of one of his puppets. Then clouds of coloured smoke would billow out from behind the stage curtains and, with a click of his long bony fingers, little flashes of lightning would spark and fizz through the fog. The Puppet Master's tall, thin frame disappeared into the smoke, making it look as if his puppets were dancing all on their own.

It was an amazing spectacle and village after village roared in delight at the performance. Their joy was soon turned to anguish, though, when they realized the price they would have to pay: one child!

I'll get you, Puppet Master, I told myself every time he took another child. *You just see if I don't.*

Silent Conversations

I hadn't been a puppet for long before I realized that the other child puppets were as alive inside their shells as I was. Although none of us could open our mouths to speak or raise our arms to signal, we *could* communicate with our eyes. Over time, using all manner of looks and blinks as a sort of Morse code, it became possible to hold a silent conversation passed from doll to doll, from one end of the caravan to the other.

I learned that some of the children had been

A few words in Puppet code.

◠◠
(⊙) (⊙) x 2 blinks = yes.

⋺ ⋲ = NO.

◡ ◡ = I don't know.

{◠◡ + ◡◠} = ssh!

◡ ◠ = I've got
an itch!

puppets for a *very* long time. I learned that Granny Green's granddaughter was called Jenny and that she was the same age as me (well, she was eight, not four hundred!), and I learned even more when the Puppet Master made his regular inspections. As he checked each puppet for damage, he used to talk in strange, one-sided conversations.

'Soon, my little friends,' he would say, 'soon, when the night is dark and cloudy, some of you will be chosen to go out on another of my secret missions. That will be fun, won't it? Will it be you, my little woodenhead, will you be the lucky one? Maybe . . . maybe not! But some of you will go out on a daring deed for your old Master.'

Go out! Go out where? What on earth was the Puppet Master on about?

Sorry, I squashed a horrible snow fly ← in my book! Yuk.

What Can I do?

I had to get away, but how? I couldn't move unless the Puppet Master pulled and twitched the cords that were attached to my hands and feet. So I had no choice but to stay where I was and watch and wait. I have no idea how long it was before I had even a chance of escape. *(I did eventually escape, of course, or this journal would never have been finished!)* But I endured many months of puppet imprisonment, and to be honest I would have preferred to be locked up in the deepest, dampest, darkest dungeon than to be trapped motionless inside my puppet skin.

Soon I learned all about the Puppet Master's 'special missions'. Sometimes he would send a few of his puppets out at night carrying burlap sacks. When they came back, the sacks clanked and jangled, and the Master emptied the contents into a big wooden chest, which he locked with a strong padlock.

If the puppets didn't return, the Puppet Master would tut-tut and curse and drive his horse on without ever looking back. I felt the anger boil up inside me. How many other children had disappeared like this? When I looked across at Jenny, I could tell by her blazing eyes that she was as angry as me.

I made myself a promise then and there, that no matter what happened, *I* was not going to remain a puppet prisoner forever; and if I had anything to do with it, neither would the rest of the puppets swinging beside me in the caravan.

In the meantime, though, I had no choice but to wait patiently for my chance to escape. I knew it would come, but I could *never* have guessed who would be responsible for helping me get free . . .

I Go On A Special Mission

We travelled beyond the valleys, over the hills and far away. I think I would have gone loopy if I'd had to put up with swinging and swaying aimlessly, clattering into other puppets and feeling dreadfully travel-sick for much longer.

After many days however, the Puppet Master pulled the caravan into a small spinney and thankfully we finally came to a halt!

The Puppet Master waited until the light had completely left the sky and it was night-time. Then, walking up and down the rows of puppets, he chose six of us, including Jenny and me. Putting us among the tools on his workbench, he unclipped the strings from our arms and legs.

'I said you would get your chance to go on a special mission, Charlie, and this is it,' said the puppeteer in his silky voice. 'You see, as Puppet Master, I can make you do anything; I could make you run and run until your joints give up and you fall into a hundred pieces; I could make you climb to the top of the highest peak and launch yourself off, believing you can fly. Or I could make you and your friends here go out on a little expedition, a shopping trip if you like, to get your old Master something he would really treasure! Ha ha!' And with that he danced an ungainly jig of joy.

Then the Puppet Master lined us up on his workbench and looked deep into our eyes. It was very quiet in the caravan. All I could hear was the gentle tick-tock of the clock on the wall. The longer I listened and the longer the Puppet Master stared into my eyes, the louder the ticking became. Soon the noise filled my head, driving out all other thoughts.

TICK-TOCK, TICK-TOCK, TICK-

My eyes became heavy and my head dropped forwards.

Message Received

The six of us sat on the bench, slumped in a dreamless sleep. The ticking of the clock echoed through my empty head and now it was joined by the Puppet Master's words, quiet but insistent, replacing my thoughts until they were the only thing I could think about.

'You will go to the house. You will find the gold. Whatever happens you will bring it back to your Master. Go to the house; find the gold; whatever happens, bring it back . . . Go to the house . . .

'. . . Come on Charlie, time to get up . . . Char-lie!'

My eyes opened and I sat up with a jolt. The Puppet Master was standing in front of me. 'Time to go, Charlie. You know what to do,' he said, with a sneer.

I knew what I *wanted* to do. I wanted to grab my rucksack, run for the door and make my escape – but I couldn't! I still couldn't move an inch on my own. The Puppet Master clapped his hands, and we all immediately stood up on the bench like a little group of performing robots. Even without our strings, we were still under his control!

'It's time. You have all been given your orders, and you have no choice but to carry them out. You are totally in my power and don't ever forget it!'

Once again I tried to move, to jump off the table and get away, but as the Master clapped his hands again, I found myself shuffling into a line with the other puppets. Help!

115

Fanlight Charlie

'Go, little puppets, go!' ordered the Master, and we moved into action; our orders swirled through our heads as we jumped down from the table, each picked up a sack from a pile by the door, and descended down the steps into the little clearing where the caravan had stopped.

We moved through the spinney, quickly crossing a lane that was bathed in moonlight, and dived into the deep shadows below the hedgerow on the far side. Pushing through the thorny branches we came to a dry-stone wall. We climbed this easily, jumping down among some trees on the other side. I had no idea what I was doing or where I was going. My arms and legs moved to the tick-tocking that still sounded in my head, driving me on against my will.

Tick-Tock, Tick-Tock, Tick-Tock...

The trees bordered a wide garden, sweeping up to a bank of ivy in front of a large manor house. It was towards this that we went, dashing across the lawn and crouching at the bottom of the bank, looking up at the dark windows of the house.

When the coast was clear, we climbed the bank of ivy. Like a little robot army, we padded quietly across to a large, pillared porch. Over the doorway was a fanlight, a semicircular window, and I waited as my puppet friends started to climb, one on top of the other, to form a human (or puppet!) ladder.

When they were ready, I started to climb this strange contraption. My arms and legs moved automatically, until I found myself standing on the shoulders of the highest puppet, who

happened to be Jenny. Using a piece of pliable material from my pocket, I slipped the catch of the window, propped it open and clambered inside.

Dropping to the ground inside the dark hallway, I slipped the bolts and let the rest of the gang in through the front door. We immediately split up, each puppet going automatically to a different part of the house.

A Fool's Gold

I padded across the hallway, up the stairs and down a dark passage. I really did try to stop and turn around, but I didn't have any choice in the matter. The tick-tocking urged me on, making my legs trot along the dark corridor and my eyes swivel behind the hard shell of my face, looking for danger. Coming to a heavy oak door, I turned the knob gently, and the door opened with the slightest of squeaks.

By the moonlight that shone through the window I saw the outline of a bed where a figure lay deep in sleep. My stiff puppet legs stepped across the room where a large

travel-trunk stood in a shadowy corner. But when I looked at it closely, my eyes bulged in terror.

I couldn't believe it! Of all the rooms in all the houses in all the world, I had been sent here! The fancy letters on the trunk

spelled out the name JOSEPH CRAIK, thief-taker extraordinaire, and my arch-enemy from my days as a pirate on the Pangaean Ocean!

How could this happen? What was the sneaky, double-crossing cheat doing here? Then I remembered what he had said to me when I had been forced to take his purse in our raid on the port of Spangelimar. '*I will follow you to the ends of the earth, Charlie Small, and when I catch you, I will see*

119

you hang,' he had said; and it looked as though he was keeping his promise! What else would he be doing here, so many miles from the sea, snoring away in a lonely house?

I wanted to turn and run as fast as I could, and I didn't want to stop until I had left the manor house, the Puppet Master and Joseph Craik far behind; but my arms and legs continued to move to the Puppet Master's will. I quietly opened the trunk, moving aside Craik's heavy coat and revealing a stash of gold underneath. There were goblets and bracelets, gold chains and a large golden crown. Craik was *meant* to be an honest thief-taker but he was obviously just one of the pirates he pretended to despise!

I quickly stuffed the gold into my sack, horrified at what I was doing, but unable to stop. When the bag was full, I sneaked back out into the corridor. I was only halfway down the passage when I heard an almighty crash coming from another room. One of the other puppets had dropped something, and the noise of it clattering down the stairs filled the whole house.

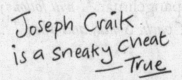

Joseph Craik
is a sneaky cheat
— True

'Wha…What's going on?' cried Craik from the room behind me. 'My gold! Someone's taken my gold!'

The next minute, he was out in the corridor and chasing after me, his pistols roaring and spitting fire!

A Crowning

I scurried along the passage, but I wasn't fast enough. In a few strides, Craik was just behind me and he dived, bringing me down in a flying rugby tackle.

I smashed to the ground, and as I did so I felt the shell-like coating around my skin crackle and craze. All of a sudden, I found that I could move my limbs by myself. I twisted and kicked against Craik's vice-like grip, and as I struggled the cracks in my shell skin got bigger. The more my skin cracked, the more I could move!

Craik shook me roughly by the shoulders. 'There's no point struggling, boy. I've got you and there's no escape,' he yelled; but with the cracking of my shell came a breaking of my bondage to the Puppet Master. I felt my own will flood through my body again! I reached into the sack of treasure and felt around inside until my hand closed on the one thing that might help me: the crown!

Craik turned me round. 'Oh boy, you're in serious trouble now,' he said with a smirk. Then he saw my face frozen in a puppet's grin and covered with a mesh of fine cracks, and his jaw dropped. 'Black-hearted Charlie?' he gasped. He seemed rooted to the spot in his shock and surprise, and this gave me my chance. Forcing my arms round, I brought the crown crashing down on his head with all my might.

It was a tight fit, but with an extra effort I pushed it down over his eyes, jamming the rim underneath his nose! Craik raised a hand to try and remove the golden blindfold, but his other hand remained on my chest,

I crowned Craik!

pinning me to the ground. Using all my
strength, I dragged myself forward and as I
pulled myself from under the weight of his
hand, I found myself squeezing out of the
puppet shell, like a snake shedding
its skin.

I scrambled to my feet,
leaving the empty husk of
my puppet self on the
floor, and shot along the
corridor.

'I will see you hang, Charlie Small,' Craik
screamed, tugging at the crown that was
jammed over his head. As I ran out onto the
landing, I looked behind me, ready to make a
cutting remark . . . and crashed straight into
Jenny, who was escaping from a different part
of the house.

'*Ooof!*' she cried, and went cartwheeling
down the wide staircase!

Oh no! I thought, threw my leg over the
banisters and slid down into the hallway below.

It was complete pandemonium. Everywhere,
ruddy-faced men in their nightshirts were
chasing the rest of the puppets, and one by one
they were all cornered and captured, their sacks

123

of booty falling to the tiled floor with a clang. All except Jenny, who was getting groggily to her feet at the foot of the staircase. There was nothing I could do to help the rest of the puppets so, seeing my chance, I grabbed Jenny's hand, ran for the doorway and we rushed out across the lawn.

All of a sudden a sash window was raised and Joseph Craik cried, 'Stop, thief!' I heard the crack of a pistol and felt the bullet as it ricocheted off the gold I still carried over my shoulder. But I kept on running! Jenny was alongside me as we reached the trees and, with one bound, we cleared the dry-stone wall to lie panting in the hedgerow beyond.

BOOF!

A Friend At Last

'Oh boy, that was close!' I gasped, looking back over the wall into the dark garden. What could we do now? I wanted to escape, to run far away, but I had no idea where we were. I looked at Jenny and found her staring at me with her dark, fierce eyes.

'*Mmmm, mmmm, mmmm,*' she said, and by the light of the moon I saw her face was criss-crossed with deep cracks. I stuck my fingernails in one chink, gave a sharp tug, and a large fragment of shell pulled away from her face.

'Ouch! Careful!' she mumbled from behind her fixed grin. I picked another piece of shell off, and another and another, and soon Jenny was moving her jaw back and forth, round and round.

'Oh, bliss!' she cried. 'I can move! Quick, Charlie. My hands, free my hands.'

I took each of her hands in mine, quickly pulling away the damaged shell and as soon as they were free, Jenny tore and pulled at the shell around her legs, scratching at her chest

until she was standing in a big pile of hard fragments and she was as free as me.

I heard the baying of a dog in the distance; it sounded as if Craik and his cronies had a tracking hound. I made a quick decision: if Jenny and I could convince the Puppet Master that we were still puppets, we stood a chance. If we stayed out in the open, we would be goners.

'We have to go back to the caravan,' I said.

'I know,' agreed Jenny. 'It's our only chance. But you need to clean your face first.'

I heard the howl of a hound

I rubbed my face and hands, and the remains of my skin-shell flaked off. When I had removed the last tell-tale signs of cracking, I put on a puppet-like grin and Jenny did the same.

'What do you think?' she asked, stepping about stiff-legged.

'Not bad,' I smiled. 'It might just work.'

Then we heard the yowls of the hound again. He had picked up our scent.

'It will have to work,' I cried. 'Let's go!'

Back Inside The Lion's Den

The Puppet Master was in a panic. He had heard the gunshots and the baying of the hound and was pacing impatiently by the caravan steps.

'At last!' he cried. 'Is it just you two?' He stared off through the trees of the spinney, but when he realized we were on our own he grabbed our burlap sacks, and lifted us up into the caravan. 'Never mind about the others, they can't talk,' he muttered to himself. 'They can't do anything!'

He opened the sack I'd been carrying and spilled its contents onto his workbench. 'Oh lovely, Charlie, you've excelled yourself,' he beamed. 'I think you and I are going to work very well together; and you too, Jenny my dear, as always. Don't worry about the other puppets, they will sit nice and quiet in a home for wayward children and no one will be any the wiser. There's plenty more where they came from!' *Poor things!* I thought as the Master quickly tied our strings back on and hung us from the beam. They'll be sent to a lock-up and no one will ever know why they don't talk and why they wander around like little lost zombies.

Luckily the Master didn't notice that we were no longer puppets. He was so excited about the gold and so aware of the dog's barking getting nearer and nearer that he didn't look too closely at Jenny and me, and we got away with our Oscar-winning impersonation.
He quickly jumped onto the driving seat and whipped his horse into a gallop and away.

This is a bit of my shell skin that I saved

The Meeting OF My Enemies

The caravan rattled down the lane and the puppets were thrown about on their strings, crashing and bashing into each other. It really hurt now that I didn't have my hard shell to protect me, and it was all I could do to stop crying out and giving myself away. We had only gone a mile or so, when somebody stepped out in front of the horse, making it rear up and forcing us to stop. I heard the bark of the hound and Craik's voice call out. 'You're in a hurry, Puppet Man. Been up to something you shouldn't have?'

'I'm giving a show beyond the marshes, and if I don't hurry I'll be late,' growled the Puppet Master. 'Now get out of my way and stop waving that pistol around.'

'All in good time,' said Craik. 'I'm looking for a nasty little pest called Charlie Small. He's wanted on both sides of the Pangaean Ocean, and less than an hour ago he robbed me of a king's ransom. I want it back, and I want to see him and his friends dangling from the end of a gibbet. So you won't mind, Mister Puppet Man, if we have a little look in your caravan, will you?'

Jenny and I stared at each other in horror.

'You don't scare me. I've never heard of Charlie Small and I don't know anything about a robbery. Now, get out of my way, or I'll run you down,' ordered the Master, his eyes blazing with anger.

'That's not very friendly, mate,' sneered Craik and all of a sudden he let off a warning shot that pierced the Master's stovepipe hat. 'The next one will trim your beard, you lanky stick insect.'

I heard the Puppet Master hiss, and with a movement too quick to see, he flicked his horsewhip, and its thin, leather tongue snaked out with a *crack!* Craik dropped his pistol with a cry, and the whip cracked again, wrapping itself around Craik's ankles. With a tug he was brought to the ground.

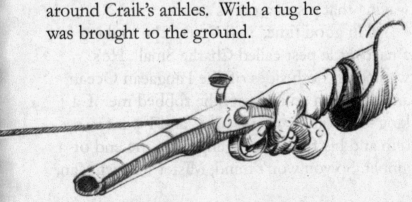

The Puppet Master urged his horse on and the caravan rumbled forwards, its heavy wooden wheels grinding the stones and just missing the thief-taker as he rolled desperately out of its path.

Soon we were thundering along the road again, the Puppet Master standing on the board at the front, his whip raised, his cloak flying out behind him and a wild look in his eye. As we raced along, the caravan jumped and bucked on the rocky road. We hit a large stone, the doors at the back of the caravan flew open and a whole show's worth of puppets were thrown out, landing in the hedgerows and ditches. The Puppet Master didn't stop; he didn't even look round, but drove the horse on even harder.

A Broken Man

We rode through the rest of the night and all through the next day. The fury of our pace never slackened until the horse, wheezing and with its coat flecked with sweat, finally slowed to a trot. The Puppet Master pulled into a roadside inn and let the animal drink its fill at the water trough.

It was then that I noticed a distinct change in the Puppet Master. Gone was the smooth, confident showman who beguiled and bewitched the public; the man that stood in front of hundreds and treated and threatened, teased and tormented them in the same breath, now crept about like a very old man. The mighty master of the puppets, the terror of every town and village in the land, who had almost glowed with energy and evil intent, was a shadow of his former self!

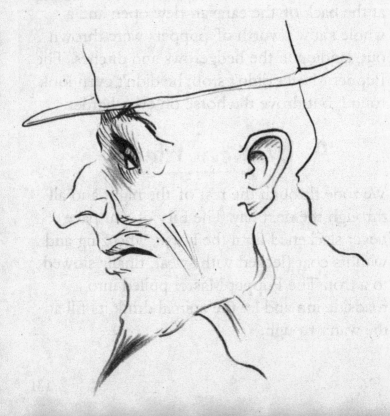

His dry limbs cracked at every movement and his grey skin had become so pale that you could almost see through it. I had no idea what brought about this change, but it had only come on after the puppets had fallen out of the caravan. Then an idea hit me like a bolt of lightning. Could it be that the Puppet Master got his power from *us*; that without his troop of performing puppets, the Master was nothing? Were we really in control of him instead of the other way around? This was something to think about...

Now that I'm able, I've been catching up on my journal. A lot has happened since I answered the Puppet Master's call and I was worried that I might get it all muddled up. So I rescued this journal from my rucksack, and while the Puppet Master has been driving the caravan on at a relentless pace, I've managed to jot everything down. Now, though, Jenny and I have a lot of work to do and plans to make. I'll write more soon.

The Puppet Master stinks

Deciding On A Plan Of Action

Hello! This is Jenny Green writing. I bet that's surprised you, but I've taken over Charlie's journal for a bit while he finds us something to eat. When I was a puppet I didn't feel like eating at all, but now I've shed my horrible puppet skin I'm absolutely ravenous!

At this very moment, Charlie is sitting high up on the shelf that runs around the inside of the caravan, rummaging through his rucksack. It was quite a spectacle to watch him get up there, almost better than going to the circus! First he pulled on his strings which were still hooked to the beam overhead and, slowly at first, he started to swing. Soon, he was swinging back and forth like a trapeze artist, whizzing higher and higher through the air.

Despite bumping and clattering into the puppets hanging around him, Charlie managed to swing level with the shelf. With one huge forward swoop, he grabbed it, and in the same movement hooked one leg onto the ledge. Then it was easy for him to scramble up, and rifle through the things he keeps in his bag.

beam

rucksack

Sorry, I can't draw very well, but this is Charlie swinging onto the shelf!
Jenny

shelf

Yum, Yum, Yum!

My tummy was rumbling and gurgling as I watched Charlie open can after can of food and wolf down the contents. As soon as he'd finished, though, Charlie filled a can with a selection of goodies and shuffling his bottom to the edge of the shelf, pushed himself off. He swung across the caravan like Tarzan swooping through the jungle, and passed me the can

of food. He was really good – it was as though he has spent half his life swinging through a tropical rainforest!

I grabbed the can and tucked in. Oh, how good it tasted! Slices of corned beef mixed with peaches in sweet syrup; cold tomato soup with croutons of Kendal mint cake. Food has never tasted so fantastic!

I'd better finish writing now as Charlie and I need to start thinking of a plan to get us out of here – if we can think of one, that is!

Bye,
Jenny.

Yum yum!

Oops, sorry!
I spilt some beans ▷

*I have a plan
Ha ha!*

It's me again – Charlie – and I think we've got a plan! I don't know whether it will work, but we've got to do something. We've noticed that some of the other puppets are so old and have been bashed about for so long that their skin is covered with a fine web of cracks. I've decided to help things along! I'll let you know how it goes as soon as I can.

Chipping Away

Days have come and gone. The scenery has changed from marsh to woodland, from plains to rolling hills, and now we are back in the land of snow and ice. Jenny and I have been very busy . . .

I discovered the little toffee hammer in my trouser pocket, which was the perfect tool to use in our escape attempt. By crawling along the beams, I slid down the puppets' strings.

With a series of sharp hammer taps, their hard
skins shattered and cracked until they
looked like jigsaw puzzles.
Then, taking my super-
sharp, super-tough croc
tooth, I chipped away
pieces of puppet skin,
exposing their real
skin underneath.
Soon it started to drop
off, and for the first time in years the children
were able to stretch their fingers and rub their
aching muscles.

    Jenny did the same, sliding along the beams
like a commando on an assault course, with my
penknife
clamped
between
her teeth.

They used my croc's tooth to cut their strings.

Jenny crawled along the beam.

'Oh, thank you so much,' whispered one of the puppets as he was freed. 'I thought I was going to be stuck here forever. Now, what are we going to do about that nasty, vicious stick insect out there?'

'Well,' I said. 'We do have a sort of plan…'

Now there are about a dozen of the children completely free. They're dangling from their strings, waiting patiently to put the plan we have been plotting into action. Oh, I hope it works! I'd better get back into my strings too. It's got to work – I just hope there are enough of us!

The Puppet Master's Home

I still can't believe what happened next. Even as I'm writing my hand is starting to shake! If it weren't for Jenny I wouldn't be here at all…

Finally one day the horse slowed its pace, and the Master steered the caravan into a long, sweeping curve. We had arrived at our destination, and I looked out of the window to try and get a glimpse of where we were. Oh, wow! I couldn't believe it; we were just entering the mouth of one of the huge Icicle Arches that I had visited before. I hoped there would be no more batty bats to deal with!

The Puppet Master drove the caravan further and further into the deep archway, until we had left the entrance far behind. We came to a halt and the Puppet Master got down and opened the doors of his caravan.

The Master had made the back of this icy cave his home. A few sticks of furniture lay dotted about; a chair and table; a cabinet where open drawers were spilling old magic tricks and coloured scarves onto the floor. A long bench stood in the corner covered in test tubes and beakers and jars of strange liquids. Was this where he concocted his potion that turned us all into puppets? I didn't have time to think about it, though. The Puppet Master pulled on a rope, some thick curtains opened behind him and the whole scene was bathed in a strong golden glow!

I squinted into the glare. It was as if the sun was rising inside the Icicle Arch; but it wasn't the sun. If anything it was even *more* incredible, because as my eyes grew accustomed to the brilliance of the glare, I understood what I was looking at: gold! Pile upon pile, and shelf upon shelf, chest upon chest and barrel upon barrel of gold. As it caught the light from the myriad icy surfaces in the cave, it reflected it back a thousandfold, turning the whole inside of the arch a brilliant yellow.

The Puppet Master's Purpose

As the curtains opened and the golden light illuminated the arch, the Puppet Master fell to his knees, raised his arms and bathed himself in the glow.

This must be the Puppet Master's whole reason for living, I thought, *to admire and polish and display his treasure.* But no matter how much loot he stole, I knew it would never be enough. He would always want more, and more and more . . . and to help him get it, he needed his army of puppets!

'Oh, what marvels! What gorgeous gewgaws and whatnots,' he cried, speaking to his treasure as lovingly as a father speaks to his child. 'I have brought some new friends for you, my pretty poppets.' He got to his feet and walked shakily over to the back of the caravan.

Come inside, Puppet Master, I said to myself. *Our plan can't work unless you do*. But he stayed outside, pulling the chest of gold to the open door and throwing back the lid. It was full to the brim, not only with Craik's gold but all the other booty stolen by the Master's puppets on his latest tour.

The Puppet Master picked up an armful of treasure and carried it over to his stash. He was very tired now and obviously weak. Then I got a shock; as he walked in front of the treasure trove, I could see the light shine faintly through his body, as if he was disappearing before my eyes. I realized, for the first time, that the Puppet Master *was not a human being*! But in that case, what kind of thing was he?

I could see
right through his body.

Showtime!

The Puppet Master carefully placed his gold in a pile. Then picking up each piece one by one, he polished it, turning it gently in his hands, before placing it lovingly in a gap on the already heaving shelves.

A spark had returned to his eye, but the Master was still weak. If we had any chance of ever defeating him, it would have to be now while his powers were low. I had to get the puppeteer back inside his caravan; *it was now or never!*

'Hey you, Puppet Master,' I called, rattling the puppet hanging next to me. 'You're heading for a fall!' I swung the puppet hard, making it clatter against its neighbour, setting it swinging and so on all down the line. The puppeteer leaped through the door like an enormous, ungainly grasshopper, and glanced fiercely around the caravan. All the puppets hanging from the ceiling were swaying to and fro.

'Where are you, you little devil?' he snarled, walking up and down the lines of marionettes, staring intently at each one. 'I'll find you, and when I do I will make you wish you'd stayed a puppet forever!'

'Where are you, you little devil?'

I waited, stony-faced, as the Master stopped in front of me, staring hard and trying to detect the slightest movement in my face. Oh boy, how I wanted to sneeze, but my life depended on me staying perfectly still. He turned to inspect the puppet opposite me, and as he did so I slipped out of my strings and dropped onto his shoulders, clamping my hands tightly over his eyes and kicking my heels with all my might. The Puppet Master stumbled, spinning round in a crazed attempt to shake me off.

'Get off, you useless piece of driftwood!' he yelled, throwing his head wildly back and forth.

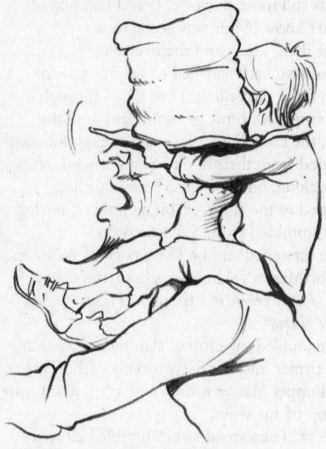

It was like trying to ride a bucking bronco.

'Yippee yi yah!' I cried in nervous excitement. 'Ride 'em, cowboy!'

Reaching up, the Master grabbed my arms and started to force them away from his face. I'm so glad he wasn't at full strength, because he was still more powerful than I had hoped. I didn't know if this was going to work!

Just then, Jenny and the twelve other children we had managed to set free rained down from the ceiling. They sliced through their strings with my penknife and hunting knife, the crocodile's tooth and the scissors, and dropped from their hooks. Some landed, biting and kicking, on the Master's back. Others dropped to the floor, grabbing hold of his legs as he stumbled around the caravan.

We scratched and bit like a pack of monkeys, but the Master's skin was as hard as a china plate. *I don't believe it!* I thought. *He's just a huge puppet himself!*

I redoubled my efforts, clamping my hands even firmer into the deep sockets of his eyes. The Puppet Master turned and span, roaring at the top of his voice.

'Now!' I screamed as he stumbled close to the doorway. One small boy crouched in front of the Master as Jenny charged from behind, shoulder-barging his legs and sending him flying through the doorway to land with a terrible crash on the icy floor below. I heard a mighty snap as the Master hit the ground and I was thrown from his shoulders and rolled across the ground. I came to a jarring halt as I banged into a stalagmite. Looking back at the Puppet Master, I was amazed to see a large crack running from his cheek, down his neck and across the top of his chest, which was now exposed by his torn and gaping shirt.

'Oh! He's hollow!' said one small boy, in a voice squeaky from not having been used for so long.

'There's nothing to him,' said Jenny. 'All this time, and he was just like a puppet himself. He's all empty!'

They were right. The Puppet Master's chest had cracked wide open and he was hollow inside, as empty as Mother Hubbard's cupboard. But, hollow or not, the evil thing was still able to scramble to his feet and, stepping forward on his long, spindly legs, he came after me. HELP!

A Snap Decision!

The hollow Puppet Master marched towards me like Frankenstein's monster. I was sprawled, winded, in front of the stalagmite, with nowhere to run. Just a few more steps and he would be on me. I had to do something.

One step . . . Think, Charlie, think!

Two steps . . . What had I got in my rucksack that might help me?

Three steps . . . I had no ideas at all!

Four steps . . . And then all of a sudden it came to me – I thrust my hand deep into my rucksack and pulled out the animal trap I had taken from Trapper Blane's hut. I forced the jaws open until the spring loader clicked, and in one movement I sent it skidding across the ice, just as the Puppet Master's foot came down.

Trigger plate

Mantrap
Set and ready to operate!

spring loaded hinge

CRACK! The jaws slammed together. The Master didn't feel a thing, but his hollow leg crumpled and he crashed to the floor once more, this time shattering like a porcelain vase into a thousand pieces. A puff of stale smoke rose from the shattered husk of his body, like the remains of an evil spell.

SNAP!

The Puppet Master's empty head, still intact, rolled across the floor and came to a halt beside me. His eyes swivelled in their sockets to look up at me.

'Charlie Small,' he hissed once, and then his eyelids closed, and his face collapsed into a pile of crumbs.

The Puppet Master's ~~head~~ head broke up into crumbs

An Unwelcome Surprise!

Now that the Puppet Master had gone, all the remaining puppets were becoming children once again. The hard shells that had imprisoned them for so long simply dissolved away. The children unhooked their strings, dropped to the floor, and poured out of the caravan into the cave.

'Hooray!' they cried when they realized the Puppet Master had gone. 'Yahoo!' As they cheered, the forest of stalactites overhead shook and shivered, clinking like huge chandeliers.

'Sssh!' I said. 'Don't yell, or we'll have that lot down on us and we'll all be speared to the ground.' The children fell silent.

'Now, let's get out of here,' I whispered.

I grabbed my rucksack, and as the roof of the Icicle Arch rattled and clinked, we made for the opening. Snow was now falling as we ran out of the arch and across the ice, reducing visibility to just a few metres.

'We've done it!' I cried, turning to the others. 'We're safe!'

But not yet! Something grabbed me from

behind. A strong hand covered my mouth and I felt a cold dagger tickling my throat.

'Where's my gold, Charlie Small?' It was Joseph Craik, and he'd brought his cronies with him. 'No tricks now, or I'll gut you like a Christmas turkey.'

Oh no, I couldn't believe it! What was he doing here? After all my hard work and all our planning, we were no better off than when the Puppet Master was alive. I had failed.

A Christmas turkey!

'It's in there,' I said angrily, pointing back into the Icicle Arch.

'Don't look so crestfallen, Charlie,' smiled Craik. 'Just look what I've got for you and your pals!' With that the thief-taker dropped a large leather hold-all onto the ground, opened the top and pulled out a series of folded metal struts, all joined together with strong elastic cords. As he unfolded them on the ground, they snapped and slotted together.

What on earth was it? I wondered, as he fixed a piece at right angles to the main upright and slotted it into a tripod of legs. *I know that shape*, I thought; *now where have I seen it before?* Then it dawned on me – I knew exactly what I was looking at. Oh no!

'Pretty nifty eh?' chuckled Craik. 'I designed it myself. A good thief-taker should always be prepared, and I did promise you that I would see you hang. I call it the Port-a-Noose! Now, when I come back with my gold, I'll let you and your pals have a go on it!'

No, no, no! I thought. This couldn't be happening. Now we were all facing the gallows!

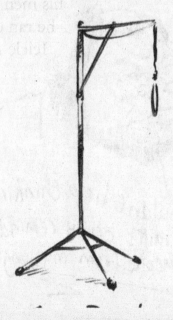

Time For A Song!

'You guard this lot, Shirley,' said the greedy thief-taker to the biggest thug in his gang.

'Shirley!' I exclaimed. 'Isn't that a girl's name?

'No it's not,' yelled the thug. 'It's a boy's name as well, so just you watch it, clever clogs!'

'Oooh! Touchy!'

'Pipe down, you,' growled Craik, raising his dagger to my throat once again. 'If this one causes any trouble, Shirley, then unbutton his belly.' He pushed me roughly towards his pal and then, beckoning the rest of his men to follow, he ran under the Icicle Arch.

I couldn't help thinking that Craik's crony reminded me of someone from my jungle days!

'This way, lads. Look at that golden glow! There must a fortune back there. What are we waiting for, mates? Let's go!'

They disappeared between the great stalagmites and stalactites that glowed with the yellow light from the Puppet Master's stash of gold. Soon their voices were lost in the depths of the cave.

The other children looked at me expectantly, but I was all out of ideas. Then, without any warning, Jenny took a deep breath and, like an opera singer, sang a note so high and clear that it cut through the air like a knife. What was she doing? Had she gone completely mad? We all stared at her, but she continued her high-pitched screech; and then as I heard the stalactites in the arch start to rattle, I realized what she was doing!

She ran out of breath, took a huge gulp of air and sang again, this time even louder.

Jenny sang!

'Argh! Stop!' cried Shirley, clamping his hands to his ears. 'That hurts!' But Jenny ignored him and the rattling of the stalactites grew louder and louder; then one by one they started to crack and shatter, falling to the ground like a thousand knives!

'Help!' Craik cried from deep inside the cave. The icicle spears fell in great swathes, slicing into the frozen ground below. *'Help!'*

Now the whole icy archway started to shake and rumble, and as Jenny's clear note continued to cut through the air, the whole mighty edifice collapsed in a roar and a huge cloud of snow. Craik's gang was gone, and the ground shook with a huge aftershock! We all stared at Jenny in disbelief.

'I used to be in the school choir,' she said bashfully.

'What have you done?' cried Shirley. 'Where's the boss gone?'

The Great Puppet Pack

He rushed towards the Icicle Arch, which was now just a large heap of snow. 'Boss, come back. Don't leave me here with all these 'orrible urchins. Boss!'

There was no reply, just the sound of the wind blowing across the snow flats. Shirley turned back to us and, pulling a heavy club from his coat pocket, advanced towards Jenny and me.

'You knew that was going to happen!' he cried. 'You did that on purpose, and now you will pay the price.'

Shirley attacks!

The other children stepped forward to surround him and try to stop his advance, but the man just laughed. With a wide sweep of his stick, he knocked them down like a row of skittles. I only had one chance. Now it was my turn to hit the right note: I threw my head back and howled and howled again and again. Shirley stopped in surprise, but as my cries faded to silence, he took another step towards me.

'Finished?' he asked, sniggering. 'I hope you feel better for that,' and swinging his club, he lumbered forward, ready to strike. Just as the club was about to crash down on my skull, we all heard a low and throaty growl.

Shirley span round, and there stood my friend Braemar, appearing from the snow-filled air like a ghostly apparition. All along a snowy ridge stood a huge pack of white wolves and, as one, they threw back their heads and howled at the sky. Craik's toughest thug panicked, and dropping his club, he turned and ran, hurried on his way by the barks of the pack and the cheers of the children.

Braemar ran and leaped forwards, knocking me back into the snow and licking my face. I rubbed his fur in gratitude and relief.

Big Shirley is a big twit!

158

'Thank you, Braemar. It's so good to see you again,' I cried. 'But what do we do now?' For, although we had defeated the Puppet Master and got rid of Craik, we were still stuck out in the middle of nowhere.

Braemar barked and the pack ran down the slope, each wolf going to a different child. Braemar turned to look at me and barked again. I knew exactly what he meant, and I climbed onto his strong, wide back.

'Come on,' I cried to the others. 'We're going home!' They all scrambled up onto the high backs of the white wolves, and Jenny climbed up onto Braemar with me. With a mighty yelp, Braemar sprinted off across the snowy wastelands, followed by the whole howling pack.

Time To Go

The sky is starting to grow light. I've been bringing my journal up to date, writing down all the ghastly adventures I had in the Puppet Master's lair. Changing into a helpless dummy and being controlled by the monstrous Puppet Man was so scary that I hope I never experience anything like it again. But I have beaten him; with the help of my friends, I have beaten him *and* Joseph Craik. HOORAY!

I've been staying at Granny Green's shop for the last week, but now I'm getting ready to leave. Everyone has been very kind to me – too kind, really. I'm being treated like a hero. If I want anything, anything at all, I only have to ask and it's mine. That's why I have to go. If I stay here much longer, I may never want to leave, and I would never see my home again. Being a hero can be really difficult. Though at first, of course, I thought it was great!

Some Hero!

Like furry white arrows, we had darted across the wastelands on our wonderful wolves, not stopping for snowstorm or nightfall. When we reached the Slate Hills, the wolves separated, each wolf taking the child they were carrying to their home.

As we galloped through the hills, we passed lines of other children, all on *their* way home. They too had been freed from their puppet prison when the Puppet Master was destroyed. They came from wherever the evil puppeteer had abandoned them. Whether it was the home for wayward children, the municipal dump or in a hedgerow at the side of some distant road, the children were on their way home at last.

Jenny and I dashed into the market square on Braemar's back, all of us howling at the tops of our voices! The villagers rushed out to see what all the fuss was and cried in delight when they saw Jenny. As the rest of the village's missing children started to arrive, Braemar licked my hand once and, before I knew what had happened, he was gone.

161

To cheers and applause, I followed Jenny as she rushed through the market square. Throwing open the door of the ironmonger's shop, she stopped, feeling awkward now she was finally home. Her grandmother became aware of the figure standing in the doorway. Granny Green's eyes filled with tears as she held out a shaking hand. The young girl rushed into her arms and they hugged and kissed and cried and calmed each other and cried again and didn't let go for a long, long time.

When Granny Green turned to look at me, I knew I had become a hero. Something, surely, that every boy would want to be, and I was no exception!

But believe me, being somebody's hero is not all it's cracked up to be.

Charlie Small is a hero! (true).

Charlie Small, Superstar!

The old woman was so pleased to have her granddaughter back that she insisted I stay with them. I was given the best room in the house and bought a new set of clothes, and after the rest of the town's children had found their way home, I could have anything I wanted. I only had to look at a toy, or a hunting knife, or a slab of bread pudding in a shop window, and immediately the grateful shopkeeper would run outside and present me with it. I was treated like royalty, and that, I'm afraid, was the problem.

I had become so famous and popular so quickly that I was in danger of becoming a bighead. My fame spread throughout the Slate Hills and beyond. I was a celebrity, a superstar, and everywhere I went, crowds followed and cheered and girls screamed my name.

I was invited to banquets arranged in my honour, and I was interviewed for all the newspapers. It was great: I was famous and I loved it. I even forgot about trying to get home. Perhaps I should stick around, I thought, and live the life of luxury.

Then one day a big-shot businessman from a neighbouring town offered me a million-dollar recording contract. He hadn't even heard me sing! I knew I had a voice like a rusty door hinge, but the man said that it didn't matter.

'We've got to strike while the iron is hot, Charlie,' he said. 'Soon you'll be yesterday's news.'

It was only when I heard myself say, 'I'm sorry, but a million's just not enough…' that I knew I had turned into a bigheaded twit. It was time to go before I made a complete fool of myself, and before Jenny, her grandmother and the whole village grew to resent me.

So now that the night is heading towards dawn; now that I've finished writing up my adventures and Jenny and Granny Green are still fast asleep, I'm going to creep downstairs, collect my rucksack and go.

I was turning into a bighead!

I have written a brief note to the old woman and her granddaughter. I didn't know how to thank them for all their kindness, so I simply wrote:

Take care of each other. Thanks for everything.
love, Charlie Small
xx

Lifting the latch on the shop door, I scampered across the square and disappeared into the alleyways that would lead me back to the open countryside and the chance of finding my own way home.

Walking The Rock-Rope

NO, NO, NO! It's all gone horribly wrong again!

I'm writing this in the shadows cast by a roaring campfire. My feet are tied tight with a thick lasso and my rucksack is too far away to get at my hunting knife and cut myself free. A coffee pot is bubbling away on the fire, and in the shadows on the other side, noisily eating his bean supper, is my captor. I can't believe I've got myself into another jam; and the day had started out so well . . .

The sun was up and it was a beautiful, clear morning. Just right for adventuring! I sucked in the crisp, clean air, whistling to keep myself company as I walked. I had no idea which way was home and could only press on, hoping that sooner or later I would recognize some familiar landmark and make my way from there. But the landscape was as strange to me as the jungle had been when I first started out on my daring escapades, and I wandered aimlessly across the rolling hills.

After some miles the landscape started to

change, becoming more rugged. Deep and jagged craters had been cut into the sides of the hills, and I realized that I was passing through an area of abandoned mine-works. Rusted pitheads stood silhouetted against the sky on top of high, scarred peaks. Huge, empty quarries that had grassed over long ago, dropped away on either side, and I found myself walking the narrow ridge between two of them.

The path that I was on became treacherous, and I whistled louder to give myself the confidence to carry on. My feet skidded, sending showers of scree sliding down the steep slopes to the quarry floor below. I knew that if I slipped, I would be cut to ribbons on the sharp stones that covered the quarry sides.

Take it steady, I told myself as the ridge started to get narrower. I got down on all fours and started to crawl, grabbing at stones that shifted and fell under my weight. I had stopped whistling now, using all my concentration to stay on top of the crumbling ridge.

Looking ahead, I could see the thin path snake out over a deep quarry to a wall of cliffs on the far side. The rock supporting the path had collapsed in the middle, so that it formed a bridge over the void below; a bridge that was no wider than my shoe. I had to stand up again, arms outstretched like a tightrope walker, and edge across, my feet feeling for the thin cord of rock.

Help! I thought as the wind blew, and I wobbled above the chasm, sweat trickling into my eyes.

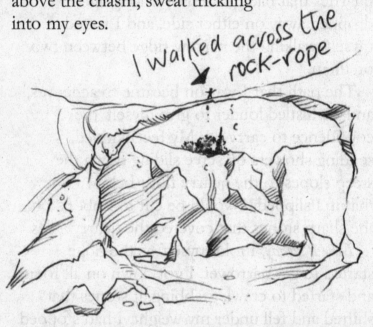

I walked across the rock-rope

The thin rock bridge beneath my feet began to crumble, shards of stone dropping into the void below. I had no choice but to go on, hoping and praying that the bridge would hold and that I wouldn't slip and fall into the rocky pit.

Eventually I made it. I scrambled across the last few feet of rock, jumped up onto the safety of the quarry's cliff top, and collapsed. Panting and shaking, I waited to get my breath back. Then, checking that I still had my rucksack, I marched off across the stony peak.

'Safe at last!' I cried, my voice echoing back from the slab-sided hills and the cavernous quarry depths.

BUT
THEN IT
HAPPENED…

Out Of The Frying Pan And Into...

With a crack-like thunder, the earth beneath my feet opened up and a huge fracture, like a bolt of lightning, snaked across the ground.

'Aaargh!' I fell into the crevice, landing on a slope of loose stones that slid away beneath me. Down I went, rolling and tumbling, until the sides of the fracture were towering above me.

Looking up, the sky seemed no more than a thin blue line. Ahead was just dust and debris, and I seemed to slide and roll for ages, until . . .

BUMP! I reached the base of the slope and came to a stop.

Looking back, I could see that I had rolled down a huge crevice that formed a gorge between two cliff walls. The ground beneath me was dusty and scrubby, and I was just about to get up and dust myself down, when I heard a familiar click behind my left ear.

'Where d'ya think you're goin', boy?' asked a soft voice. I turned around carefully, with my arms raised, and found myself staring down the barrel of a Colt.45. 'Oh, shucks! It's a bad day for you, boy,' smiled the young man, staring back at me with his clear blue eyes. 'You've just barged into the camp of Wild Bob Ffrance, the most wanted outlaw in the whole of the wild west!'

Oh no! What am I going to do now?

PUBLISHER'S NOTE
This is where the third journal ends.

By hook or by crook, we'll be last in this book

from

Jenny X

and

Granny Green. X

Good luck Charlie we hope you get home safely.